# THE VANISHED SPECIALIST

*LOST PLANET SERIES: BOOK TWO*

USA TODAY BESTSELLING AUTHOR

# K WEBSTER

NEW YORK TIMES & USA TODAY BESTSELLING AUTHOR

# NICOLE BLANCHARD

Mandy,
♡ K ~~~~~

Nicole Blanchard

*The Vanished Specialist*
Copyright © 2019 K Webster & Nicole Blanchard

Cover Design: IndieSage
Photo: Shutterstock
Editor: Emily Lawrence
Formatting: IndieSage

# CONTENTS

My lilapetal is dying...and I can't save her.
The woman who brought me back to life may not live long enough to see me truly happy.
All the tests, the experiments have failed me...and I have failed her.
If I don't devise a cure to save my alien, I'll spend the rest of my existence on Mortuus alone.

The others believe my mate isn't strong enough to survive. That she can't breed and should be put back into cryosleep until she's healed.

But I won't allow it.

I will defy the only family I've ever known to save her. Even if it means vanishing into the unknown.

She is all that matters and no amount of her protests will keep me from doing what I must to keep her safe.

In the beginning, there were many who survived the initial blasts of radiation and the resulting catastrophic environmental disturbances. The morts, the only inhabitants of Mortuus, The Lost Planet, ever changed from the effects of the radiation, learned to adapt and, more importantly, to survive. In doing so, they became highly skilled and intelligent, capable of surviving even the worst conditions.

The planet was dangerous and life wasn't easy, but the morts had each other and that was all that mattered. They flourished in the protective shell of an abandoned building they converted into living quarters. Morts were given jobs, trained from birth in order to pass knowledge from generation to generation.

Eventually, the morts hoped to extend the facility and conquer the wild, untamable outdoors.

Then, disaster struck.

The Rades, a disease contracted from complications of the radiation, began to infect increasing numbers of their population. First, there was fever, followed by sores, then finally madness and, inevitably, death. Quarantining the infected helped, but by then it was too late. Women, children, and the elderly, were the first to go. One by one, morts caught The Rades and died. Whole families wiped away.

Until only ten males remained.

Salvation came years later when the morts discovered a ship filled with aliens—female aliens. Knowing it was their only chance at survival, they snuck on a passing ship and brought the females home to study—and to breed.

Two females have been claimed. Three remain.

From my vantage point, I can see straight into the sub-faction. She—Emery, as they say—is so fragile. Like the fine petals of a lilabush. But unlike the healthy flowers that grow in Galen's lab, this one wilts. With each passing solar, her skin grows more pallid. The tiny coughs rattle from her chest and her breaths come out labored.

Aria, the commander's mate and leader of the human sub-faction, has been distracted creating the home for the humans and readying the space for the others to be woken up, but she is overlooking the needs of my lilapetal. She is letting her die before our very eyes.

As usual, when I'm stealing gazes of Emery, her yellow-haired nog will slowly turn and seek me out.

She does not smile for she is too weak. She does not gesture in greeting. All she does is cry. Silently. Motionless. The tears I've tasted while she was in cryosleep were unlike anything my forked tongue has ever had the pleasure of licking. I crave to hold her in my solid arms and lick away her sweet sadness.

But I am not allowed to hold her.

Aria demands I keep my distance until Emery can decide these things for herself. They do not understand I've studied her expressions long before she became the next awoken one. I feel attuned to her. She coughs and sputters, and yet I do not fear the pathogens that litter the air around her. It is unimportant to me because her well-being trumps all. The idea of anyone else coughing like that is enough to have me running back to the lab and sitting under the equalizer to eliminate the bacteria.

Emery, I'd gladly catch whatever it is she ails from.

Then I could hold her while it stole us both from this life.

Nobody, especially Emery, deserves to die alone.

I won't rekking allow it.

With my eyes locked on hers, I try to read her expressions. She's sad but mostly worried. Using what little energy she does have, she tugs and twists at the zuta-metal that is around her arm. I feel like it unlocks an important secret about her. I've scoured through the test results Avrell has obtained from her and read through his notes.

For someone so brilliant, our faction's physician is plagued with not knowing what to do.

There's a name for her ailment. She spoke it to Aria and it's been recorded, but it means nothing to us morts. Asthma. Inhaler. All we know is her lungs struggle even on her own planet, but at least there she had the proper medicine. She is too weak for us to try to send her back. It's been discussed. With space's compression on one's lungs, she would not survive. That is written in Avrell's notes as well.

Which means...

There is only one thing left to do.

I study contagious diseases and pathogens. I find cures for our people. It's what I'm good at. Like second nature. This will be no different. I won't stop until I've done it.

I will cure her.

Quietly, I step into the sub-faction and stalk her way, thankful that Hadrian, our youngest and most talkative mort, is nowhere to be seen. Her eyes widen in surprise, but she does not call out. Something that resembles relief flashes in her bright blue eyes. It's enough to fuel me forward on my mission—a mission that'll no doubt get me locked away in a reform cell, should Breccan and the others intercept it.

I cannot fail.

Kneeling beside her, I hover my palm over her cheek, desperate to touch her. But Aria's commanding words still ring in my nog. Her laws about only touching if they ask. Hesitation swirls inside of me like the stirrings of an epic geostorm.

"Help me," Emery croaks out, her body shuddering slightly as she pleads. "Help me or I will die."

I allow my palm to stroke the side of her face—and then I do the unthinkable.

I gently pull my fading alien into my arms, careful not to break her, and carry her out of her new home.

With haste, I rush back to my lab, where I will lock us away. They'll find us eventually, but I will have to make sure they can't get in. I'll work relentlessly, undisturbed by them, until I find a cure.

I *will* rekking save her.

"Relax now, lilapetal," I urge, my voice soft, just for her. "I'm going to heal you."

Or I'll die trying.

IT'S DARK, *the room where they lead us and the hallway*
*beyond. It makes me shiver even though it's warm*
*enough to make the bodies around me emit the rank,*
*sour scent of sweat. The thin, threadbare gown they*
*gave us does little to contain body heat, so I try to wrap*
*my arms around my waist and get a sharp jab in the ribs*
*for attempting to struggle through the handcuffs I forgot*
*I was wearing.*

*They file us in, one by one, and with each step*
*closer to the yawning doorway that will lead me to my*
*fate, my chest squeezes tighter and tighter. I know*
*mentioning my need for an inhaler will fall on deaf*
*ears, so I try to control my breathing, remembering the*
*techniques my mother taught me.*

"Relax, Emery. Listen to the sound of my voice."

*The sound of her words is faint, has gotten more and more so in the years since she passed away, and it does little to drown out the sound of the others' weeping or the guards' sharp directives. My breath wheezes and spots dance across my vision as the line of us moves closer to the door.*

*I don't know where we're going and I wouldn't dare to ask, even if I could get the words around my labored breathing. The last one who tried to speak got a vicious backhand for her troubles. I have enough problems without drawing attention to myself.*

"Breathe, little one. You have to breathe."

*It's my turn. The guard beside me shoves me through the doorway and my lungs seize as I stumble forward. A scream catches in my clenched throat and I fall.*

I jolt awake, my lungs and body both aching. A pair of strong arms are around me and I glance up at the concerned—or at least I think it's concerned—expression of the alien who took me from where I was resting. My legs are wrapped around his waist, his hands warm at my back. I must have fallen asleep on the trek from the rooms where Aria was keeping me.

He shifts all my weight to one brawny arm, somehow managing to balance as he walks, and brings his free hand to press against the juncture of my throat.

"Breathe, little one. You must relax or the commander and his mate will surely rekking send me to The Eternals, skinned and butchered like a rogcow."

I struggle to do as he directs, my stubborn lungs fighting me with every inhale. I was dreaming. It was just a dream. I focus on the sound of his soothing words to clear away the cold press of fear.

"That is it," he says, adjusting me again until I'm snug against his chest. "We are almost there."

The one the others call Calix is the only thing about my new reality that doesn't frighten me. He should. He's nearly seven-foot tall with ghost-white skin and jet-black, close-cropped hair. His size alone should be intimidating, even if he weren't an alien. But he also wears glasses that are currently balanced precariously on the edge of his nose and there's a tablet stylus tucked behind one of his pointy ears. If he were an awful alien or monster, he wouldn't look so... normal. Something about him put me instantly at ease, more so than any male I've ever come in contact with—this planet or elsewhere.

"There? Where are we going?" I ask breathlessly. My cheeks are raw with the remnants of my tears. I want to scrub away the sign of my weakness, but I can barely hold on to his neck as it is.

His arms tighten around me. "I am taking you to

my lab. You will be comfortable there and it will give us time to heal you. Do not worry, my lilapetal, I will not fail you."

The farther we get from the bustle of the main building, the more my chest eases. I take comfort in his presence. Enough that my breathing begins to settle as I become distracted by the melodious lilt of his voice. I could listen to him talk forever. "Lilapetal?"

The length of his long, clawed fingers tangle in my hair in soothing strokes, then return to my waist. "A flower, delicate, one of the only to survive the harsh climate here on Mortuus. It is elegant and beautiful, but strong. It reminded me of you the moment I saw you."

"That's so sweet of you to say."

We reach a door and Calix shifts my weight to wave an armband. The door opens with a swish and we stride through.

"Good solar, Calix. How may I assist you?" a digitized female voice greets.

"Silent mode," he grunts out. Then to me, he says, "Uvie. She is a computerized program that we use when we need assistance with our duties. I will not require her assistance this solar."

Opposite the doorway, I see our reflection in a row of tall glass-fronted cabinets. Even from a distance, I wince at the reflection of my pale face. It almost blends in with the snow-white color of his skin. My hair hangs in limp strands, the once bright blond locks knotted and unwashed from the long stay in the cryotube and then in the sub-faction, as they called it, barely able to move once I was woken up.

He carries me past a long work table scattered with what looks like notebooks, beakers filled with unidentifiable liquids, and a smattering of papers to one of three doors that open to reveal an examination room of sorts—a bed, machines nearby, and medical-looking tools. Calix places me on the somewhat stiff bed with extra care, his dark eyes roving over me with an emotion akin to tenderness. Simply being away from the chaos of the other rooms has improved my ability to breathe. I've only been awake at this *facility* as Aria calls it for a few days, but it's already claustrophobic with all these people. Their commander named Breccan is always growling and making Aria giggle, which oddly enough, annoys the heck out of me. Avrell, their doctor, is friendly, but always poking and prodding at me. And Hadrian is so talkative and extremely exhausting.

Here, it's quiet and peaceful. Calix even shut up the computer lady.

A voice inside my head tells me maybe this brawny

alien has something to do with the calmness I feel, but I brush the thought away. That's impossible. I barely know him.

"How are you feeling?" he asks as he drags a screen on an extendable arm down to the bedside. It comes to life with a *whir* as he retrieves his stylus and begins writing.

"Better, for now. Thank you for helping me."

He pauses, his pen hovering above the screen, and I can feel his eyes moving over me like a physical caress. The silence extends for a moment longer, then his pointy ears twitch and the briefest flash of a forked tongue appears as he licks his lips. "Think nothing of it, lilapetal. I am going to begin by taking your stats and then we will get you cleaned up."

I jolt upward, despite the effort it takes to lift my head. "You aren't going to...I dunno, start? Tests or procedures or whatever."

I'd been to the doctors so many times for my asthma, I'd gotten used to being treated like an experiment rather than a person. Even with Aria and Avrell, they discussed me like a project. Something to do, to fix. With Calix, it's not like that, it would seem. He wants to help me, but when he looks at me, it's almost like he truly sees *me*. After being invisible for so long, being caught in his gaze is like being warmed from the inside out.

Heat blooms inside me and I try not to melt under his stare.

He's this...thing...and yet, I'm attracted to him in a way I can't seem to understand. Truth be told, I like the spell he seems to have me under. It distracts me from everything else that's not pleasant.

He lifts a hand and cups my cheek, the tips of his claws lightly scratching over my flesh. "I think you have had enough shocks to your body for a time. You have undergone a trauma and you will heal better once you have been groomed and changed into clean coverings. After that, you need to rest. While you sleep, I will run blood panels and do scans with my instruments. You will not feel a thing."

I have to admit, clean clothes and a shower will do wonders. As he resumes his note-taking, I recline on the bed and attempt to let him work, which lasts all of two minutes. "Why are you helping me?"

"It is my duty," he tells me, his eyes not meeting mine.

"This goes beyond the call of duty," I say back, nudging for more information.

"I suppose it does." Calix attaches a band to my

arm, his fingers lingering on my skin before meeting my stare with a sad expression of his own. "Some time ago a deadly disease affected our people." His eyes grow distant as though he's seeing something I can't. "It took most of our kind. There are only ten of us left now. There were several strains of various diseases after our planet was ravaged by radiation. It took our families swiftly and without discrimination. After my mentor succumbed to the disease, I was all who was left to try and stop it from spreading." His features darken as he remembers. "I could not stop it, though, despite all my training, despite all the knowledge I have gained. All we can do is keep the ones inside this facility safe and those harmful pathogens out. I will not let you succumb to something trying to take your life...I cannot. I will help you like I could not help those others. All life is precious and needs to be protected. Even yours, sweet alien."

I cover his hand and it stills beneath my touch. Despite his unusual appearance, my curiosity about his past is undeniable. After the hell I survived, his gentleness soothes the wounded parts of me. The kinder he is to me, the more my need to be around him —for *him*—grows. Even now, he watches patiently for my answer and I want to lap up his gentle responses from the source. "I'm sorry you had to go through that, Calix."

His lips firm into a line, his ears twitching. "Do not be sorry, little one. My troubles are not your burden to bear. Rest while I finish taking your stats. It will not be long."

It's strange to feel safe. And for once in a long time, I do. On my own planet, it wasn't exactly easy after my mother died. And then...

My mind drifts to my captors. The cold ship. Their even colder glares. A shiver runs down my spine. At least these people—despite clearly not being human —seem *more* human than the ones I was with last. I dart a glance at his dark eyes as he works. His brows are furrowed in concentration. A very humanlike expression contorts his face.

Definitely safer.

Especially with Calix.

Miraculously, or perhaps because the past few days have taken their toll on my body, I do as he instructs and relax. As he works, my mind wanders to all the information Aria has tried to cram into my brain when I first woke up.

We're on a horrible planet. The terrain, the atmosphere, the creatures, the pathogens. It's amazing these morts as she calls them have survived this long. But the aliens here are good, she claims. From what I've learned of them and now with Calix,

I can see that. No one has tried to harm me. Not like...

I blink away those horrible thoughts and focus on the now. Here. This facility. Aria told me about all the alien guys here. I haven't met them all. Her guy is Breccan—the commander. He's big and grumpy. Not sure why she likes him, but she's carrying his baby nonetheless. Hadrian is younger than the others and is like her assistant. Avrell is the doctor, and apparently Calix is kind of like their scientist. There's another one named Draven, who sort of creeps past the doorway to the sub-faction, but never enters. Some of the other names run together and I can't remember them all. Another one I remember, though, is Sayer. Aria explained how he's a linguistics genius and has somehow implanted a translator into the other morts' heads that allows them to understand hundreds of languages, including ours. Not only do they under-stand them, but it helps them reply back in the language they're spoken to in.

The sound of the humming from the machines and the muffled tap of his stylus against the screen lull me into a light doze, this time thankfully void of terrifying dreams.

When I wake again, it's to the sound of rain—or at least that's what it sounds like. I crack open an eye and find myself once again in Calix's arms. I could get used to being carried around like precious cargo.

"What are you doing?"

He sets me down on my feet and moves to a dimly lit closet he illuminates with a press of a button. Water spurts from the ceiling with the press of another. "I have finished my examination. Our cleansing unit will help rejuvenate you. I have programmed it for a gentle wash and scrub and I will have your minnasuit ready for you to change into."

"Minnasuit?" I ask as he hovers by the door.

He gestures toward me. "Minnasuit. Dress?" His cheeks go adorably dark. Not with red like mine would, but almost with shadow, which I assume is his version of a blush.

"Clothes?" I say around a smile.

When he smiles back at me, I lose my breath. Except this time it has nothing to do with my faulty lungs. It could be because the double fangs he's sporting are, to put it lightly, fucking intimidating, but in a sexy way. A way that makes me curious about how they'd feel if I were to kiss him. They give a wolfish edge to his otherwise handsome face that I find undeniably attractive, alien or not. "Yes, clothes. I forget what Breccan's mate calls them. If you need anything else, I will be just outside."

15

He turns to leave and I take a step forward. "Calix."

"Yes?" he says over his shoulder.

"Will you..." I feel silly saying it and I almost tell him never mind, but somehow this new Emery, the one who rose from the cryotube after she thought it was the end, is braver, more willing to take chances. "Will you stay? Close, I mean. I don't want to be alone."

I'd been alone for so long, after losing my mother, it didn't even occur to me to focus on the fact he wasn't human. If it were any of the big guys, like Breccan or that scary one, Draven, who I'd seen poking his head in here and there, I'd be running in the opposite direction, but there's a part of me that recognizes Calix on a deeper level. A part that doesn't want him to go anywhere. Maybe it's because he knows how to heal me, but I don't think that's it.

I need someone who cares about me and for the first time in ages, I finally feel someone does. And I want it so badly, I'll do anything for that feeling, even for just a few more stolen moments. Even if that need scares the hell out of me.

"I will be here," he says. "I am not going anywhere."

We lock eyes for one long moment—a connection

seemingly crackling through the air and tethering us together—before he steps through the door. When he closes it behind him, I wish I knew how to adjust the temperature of the water. I need a cold shower after the way he looked at me.

Hot. Intense. Possessive.

Something tells me the chill of the water will do nothing to cool the heat burning through me now.

[ 2 ]
CALIX

I HAVE HER.

I rekking have her.

Breccan is going to beat me in the nog, but I do not care. Consequences are meaningless when her health is in a delicate balance.

While she bathes, I pace my lab. There is so much I want to do. So much I need to ask. I am going to figure out what is wrong with her and correct it.

I consider myself a fairly reserved and calm mort, but rekk if Emery does not seem to spark my inner flame. Now that she is not only in my presence, but also under my care, I am burning from the inside out with the need to protect her.

She is mine.

I shake my nog because those possessive thoughts

will only cloud my thinking. And this solar is important. We are about to embark into unknown territory. I have spent many revolutions studying our people. Being our faction's contagious disease specialist, I am responsible for knowing the ins and outs of every potentially harmful condition that could affect our people.

It is the aliens whom we know nothing about.

My mind seems to throb inside my nog—pulsating with the need to know and understand. It is not a matter of if with my sunray-colored haired alien, but when. I will find out what is ailing her and I will heal her.

I just hope it is not too late.

*Like them.*

The thought is violent and I suppress a shudder. Not a solar goes by where I do not mourn the losses of the ones I could not protect. The Rades is a disease that destroys our people from the inside out. And no matter how long I have studied it, I can never come up with a cure. Since there is no treatment and the mortality rate is high, we do our best to prevent it. Cleanliness is of utmost importance. We are wary and watchful of any early signs of the disease. We do what we can, but it will never be enough. Tirelessly, I search for a cure for that wretched disease that could rear its ugly nog at any moment. And as much as that disease claws at my every thought, fixing Emery takes precedence.

I will cure her, even if it is the last thing I do.

The water shuts off in the cleansing station and awareness prickles through me. I imagine her naked and with water sliding down over her pink curves. I am curious about her body. Breccan seems quite enamored with Aria, that is for certain. I would be a liar if I said I was not enamored either. Not with Aria, but with the idea of Aria. A female. One who Breccan was allowed to breed with. Their physical connection morphed into what our parents had, long before everything broke apart. Families were special and to be revered. For so long, though, the only family we have had was each other.

Now we have *them*.

Aria and Emery and the other aliens.

With Aria, we have a future.

Images of Emery's stomach swollen with my mortyoung has the possessive beast inside of me once again raging. I want her. Everything in me craves to touch and taste every part of her. I want what Breccan has. But not with just any alien.

With Emery.

The idea of any other mort rutting against my

lilapetal has my vision turning red with rage. I am not typically one to get angry like Draven or Breccan, but when it comes to Emery, I am out of control. My emotions run rampant like a heard of rogcows being chased by a pack of sabrevipes.

*Swooosh.*

The panel of the door slides open and there she stands. Delicate and shivering, dressed in nothing but a drying cloth wrapped around her body that she clutches to keep closed. Her normal shade of pink has become dark with a hint of blue. Especially her bottom lip. The lip I have carefully dragged my claw along while she slept so many solars. My feet carry me her way, eager to touch, to assist, to rekking breathe her in.

My alien does not cower and that has pride thumping inside me. I remember how skittish Aria was at first. She was not brave like my lilapetal.

"The minnasuit, er, clothes?" I ask, my voice raw and husky. My fists are clenched tightly at my sides, my claws digging into my flesh almost hard enough to break the skin.

"I was..." She staggers forward. "I wasn't feeling too well—"

Her body collapses in front of me and I catch her before she careens to the floor. Panic rises up inside of me. Time is of the essence. I need to study her and test theories. I need to rekking fix her.

I slide my arm beneath her thighs and lift her. The drying cloth does nothing to hide her perfect skin from my curious eyes. Carrying her back over to the examination table, I greedily allow my gaze to rove over her as I turn on the warming lights. Her bluish lips are parted and her purple eyelids are fluttering. The drying cloth has fallen away to reveal her delectable breasts to me. Each nipple is peaked and if her health was not in dire need of attention, I would spend a lot more time inspecting them.

Once I settle her down on the heated table, I allow the towel to fall away. Her cunt shines with golden sunray hairs that match that on top of her nog. I snag a warming sheet and cover her body with it. I am tempted to call in Avrell, but then he would see her like this. So vulnerable and broken. She does not trust them like she does me. I have not earned her trust, but I will not let her down. Besides, I know everything Avrell knows. We studied the same and have worked together on countless endeavors. I am confident that if anyone can help her, it is me.

Her breathing is raspy and uneven. It unnerves me, but I do not let it affect me as I attach a breathing apparatus to her nose and mouth. The machine pumps oxygen into her brittle lungs and within minutes, her pink coloring returns. Her eyes open and she regards me sleepily.

Blue. Curious. Unafraid. Sad.

I become lost in her stare. So brave, yet so weak. One of the universe's mysteries.

Reaching forward, I drag a claw over her cheekbone gently. The corner of her lips twitches with the briefest of smiles. It's enough to stoke the flames inside of me.

"Please rest, my Emery. In order for me to understand your ailments, I will need to study you. Listen to your breathing. Take more samples. It is important," I tell her as I attach some sensors to her upper chest near her heart and one at her pulse point.

*Beep. Beep. Beep.*

Her pulse is slow but steady.

She gives me a slight nod but does not close her eyes. Instead, she scrutinizes my every move. I have never had anyone watch me with such intensity. Hadrian has studied under me often, but the mortarekker can't keep still long enough to notice details.

Emery sees them all.

Intelligence glimmers in her eyes that have been dulled by illness.

I vow to make them shine again.

Using the wegloscan wand, I wave it over her stomach and am secretly grateful when it blinks red, indicating she is without child. If she were to be impregnated like Aria, one of the other morts might think he had claim over her.

All of the aliens were implanted with embryos. On a routine mission to orbit our planet, Theron and Sayer managed to get inside a passing vessel and procured the cryotubes. All five were carrying females inside in cryosleep. It brought hope to our faction because, for once, we could breed and our race was no longer threatened with extinction. Avrell worked hard to implant the aliens with our seed. He used samples from all of us morts, hoping that some would stick. There would be no need to wake them or physically mate with them. However, Aria's never took and she woke from cryo miscarrying. It was not until she mated physically with Breccan that they were able to conceive. I know because of their mating, she is now growing a little mortyoung in her womb. I have seen the hungry looks in the other morts' eyes. Hungry for the only other alien who is awake.

She is mine.

Amusement glitters in her eyes and it is then I realize I am growling.

Embarrassment washes over me and I swallow down the strange feeling.

"You're not pregnant," I tell her. I am sure Aria has explained things to her, but it is no less frightening.

Her eyes widen and they dart back and forth, panicked. I grab her shaking hand in mine and run my nose along the back of it as I inhale her clean scent.

*Beepbeepbeepbeep!*

"I will not let anyone touch you," I whisper against her flesh, searing her with a firm stare. "Relax, lilapetal."

She must find assurance in my expression because her heart rate slows and she relaxes.

"Just breathe normally. I'm attempting to repair your lungs with microbots again. I hope they will tend to any damages they are capable of fixing."

I do not tell her that the microbots have not been programmed for alien anatomy, but perhaps it is best if she does not know the details. I locate my audonar that is used for listening inside the chest and slide the small bulbs into my ears. Using the round zuta-metal disk that is attached by a tube, I press it to her pink flesh above where her heart is. Our eyes meet as I listen to the steady thumping.

Once I am satisfied with the sound of her heart, I slide the disk over to have a listen to her lungs. The heel of my palm brushes against her peaked nipple and she lets out a mewl. The small, sweet sound speaks straight to my cock. I grow hard in my minna-suit and I am once again shamed by my response to her.

"Try and remain calm, lilapetal." My words are gruff and I hope she does not realize how desperate I am to mount her and claim her as mine. "That is it," I rumble. "Breathe just like that."

Her eyes are sharp and focused as she burns her hot gaze into me. Pink colors her throat and for a moment I worry I have hurt her. Then, I realize what my thumb is doing. I'm stroking her in a comforting way. Each time my thumb moves from left to right, my claw slides across her breast just below her nipple over the warming sheet.

I freeze and jerk my eyes back to hers, expecting something angry to glimmer in her stare. Aria was always so angry.

But not my Emery.

Her blue eyes are soft and trusting.

"Are you feeling okay to breathe without the apparatus?"

She nods and I quickly pull it away, eager to hear her voice once more.

"If ever I do something you feel uncomfortable

with, please express your displeasure," I say, my words husky.

Her shaky hand finds mine and she covers it with her own. "You're helping me. I've met a lot of bad people in my life, and, Calix, you're not one of them."

Out of habit, my thumb strokes her flesh again. "I want to cure you."

She smiles sadly. "I don't think you can, but I'm happy that you're trying."

Pride surges through me as I continue to listen to her chest. It is as though someone poured something thick and sticky into her lungs. They seem to crackle as she breathes.

"So you suffered from this where you came from?" I ask as I pull away the audonar disk and pull the bulbs from my ears. I cannot imagine trying to breathe with lungs that seem to want to glue shut with every breath. How terrifying her life must be.

"Yeah. Asthma was something I grew up with. My inhaler helped, but there was nothing that completely healed me." Her brow furrows and I crave to smooth it out again. "I did what I could to keep from having an asthma attack, but sometimes it was inevitable." She twists the zuta-metal bracelet around her wrist. "This, where I came from, let people know I have a condition and would need immediate treatment if I ceased breathing. Now, though...I'm a walking time bomb. There must be something in the air here my lungs find even more offensive than back home."

I blink at her in confusion, unsure what a walking time bomb is. "I am going to draw some blood and urine samples. I'd like to study your bionetics."

"Bionetics?"

"It is a unique formula. Each mort here has a different bionetic formula. Aria's is different as well. I have samples from Aria and I would like to run them against yours."

"Whatever you need to do, I'll do it," she murmurs.

I work diligently taking the samples from her. When it comes time for the urine sample, she bravely meets my stare as I aid her in sitting on the collection basin. She urinates, her cheeks flashing red, but clutches onto my shoulders as though I will catch her if she should fall.

"This is awkward," she complains, her breath tickling my hair on my nog.

Awkward. I remember the word that did not translate for us well. Aria uses it a lot. It means uncomfortable.

"Ahh, but it is necessary, my sweet."

She smiles, broad and bright. The flame that had been kindling inside me has exploded like that of the harmful sun in our sky. I can see why Breccan craves it with every fiber of his being.

"Lie back," I instruct as I pull away the basin and set it on the table. Absently, I cleanse her between her thighs.

Swipe. Swipe. Swipe.

Small, needy sounds escape her and I jolt from my stupor.

"I apologize," I croak out as I regretfully pull my hand from her cunt. "I only wanted to make sure you were clean."

My cock is swollen and hard in my suit. Lies. I became enraptured in her pink folds and golden hair. I enjoyed touching her.

"It's okay," she assures me, her voice shaking. "I liked it."

I blink at her in confusion. She likes when I cleanse her or... Based on the way her neck turns bright red, nearly the color of the aliens' blood—which we've learned is brighter and less black looking than our own—and how she bites on her bottom lip, I would say she means something else altogether.

She liked it when I *touched* her.

Memories of nights where sleep wasn't even an option flood through me. Nights where I would run my fingers along her smooth flesh that was available to me as she lay in the cryotube. The way, even in her sleep, sweet whimpers and glimpses of smiles were gifted to me.

She squirms on the table and it is then I get a scent.

A scent so sweet and decadent, it speaks to every fiber of my being.

Arousal.

Another growl rumbles through me and my eyes sear into hers.

"I need to study these samples," I croak, my gaze never leaving hers.

"Okay." Her bottom lip wobbles and tears well in her eyes. The dulled blue transforms into the color of the glassy stones we sometimes mine from the underground caves.

Stunning.

"I...I..." I start but trail off. "Should I continue to, er, cleanse you there? I don't want to make you sad."

A tear leaks out and she gives me a small nod. "I, uh, I just...it felt good and I've been denied anything good for quite some time."

I drag the small wet cloth back to her cunt and swipe it between her folds. Her body jolts and her flesh rises with bumps. My chest contracts as I worry that she is reacting badly to the touch.

"Just use...don't use this," she whispers as she pulls

away the cloth and sends it fluttering to the floor at my feet. Her hand, small and icy, grips my wrist. "This. Use this."

I rise from my chair and it rolls out from beneath me. My cock is aching in my minnasuit and I'm thrumming with need. She is so fragile and suffering. Who am I to deny her a small pleasure?

Rekk, who am I trying to fool?

I'll give her any rekking thing she asks for.

Even this.

Aria will be maddened if she finds out.

"Perhaps we should not," I say, hating the words as they tumble past my lips.

Her frown is my undoing and I find myself heeding to her sweet unspoken demands without further argument. I run my claw along her slit, reveling in the way her body jolts. Intensity burns in her gaze and this is the first time since she was awoken that she looks alive. Truly alive. Using my other hand, I greedily rove my palm across her hip bone and pull aside one of her folds. I'm curious to see what hides inside.

A small bud.

Pink and swollen.

Like that of a lilapetal.

I wonder if it smells sweet, too.

Retracting my thumb claw, I rub along the bud. She arches her back and sputters out a moan mixed with a cough. I panic, but then she urges me on.

"More, Calix."

Another growl rumbles from me as I give her little bud more attention. Her arousal becomes heady in the air. It is so thick I could bottle it up and inhale it later. I watch her expressions, listen for her sounds, and take note of the way her body moves. Quickly, I learn what makes her feel good.

She climbs and climbs and climbs.

So many times, I have climbed that same steep slope. Alone, in my quarters. My hand wrapped around my thick length. Imagining my own little alien naked and squirming beneath me. I would spill and spill. Over and over again. But I was always alone. There was never a fall, just the lonely climb.

Yet, now?

Together, we climb.

Up, up, up.

The pleasure I felt physically now saturates every part of my insides. Like I'm infected with a disease, but one I would gladly die from.

She reaches her delicate hand my way and I groan when her fingertips graze along my aching cock in my minnasuit. Her movements match the way I touch her. Frantic and desperate.

Climb and climb and climb.

A croaked moan rattles from her and it lures out a groan of my own. Her body silently shudders as my seed spills unapologetically into my minnasuit. There is no room for shame as our eyes greedily seek out the other.

Fall and fall and fall.

Together we fall.

Into something.

We'll never be alone again.

# [ 3 ]
## EMERY

I CAN'T BREATHE, but for once, it doesn't scare me and send me into a panic that only worsens the symptoms. Instead, I'm calm...happy. He scurries off to a closeted area. I hear some running water and some shuffling before he returns wearing a new skintight suit that accentuates how well-endowed he is.

It's a struggle, but I sit up to get a better look at him, wrapping the warm sheet over my shoulders. Calix's hands stroke down my body as it still quakes with aftershocks. He whispers nonsensical sweet words into my ear and I turn my face into his neck, my hand diving into the thick scruff of his close-cropped hair. He doesn't keep it long, like the others. Not my sexy scientist. He inches back, his dark eyes locked on mine, and I lift a hand to trace the pronounced edges of his cheekbones, the bony ridges of his prominent brow.

When he doesn't object, I tug him closer, lifting to fit my mouth to the firm curve of his, pressing a kiss to his lips. Despite the orgasm he's just given me, I find myself pulling closer, my breathing labored, hoping for him to deepen our kiss, but he doesn't. In my world, I'd never been bold. My sickness had left me on the sidelines of my own life. I watched instead of participating. I'd observed instead of experiencing.

I've been the one receiving orders instead of giving them. Calix is all too happy to follow my lead and the power of being in charge is intoxicating. He's so different, so kind, to me. When he touched me between my legs, I wasn't shy. I was...bold. The kind of woman I always wanted to be. So when I see my own need reflected in his eyes, I ask for the one thing I never wished for back in my old life...more.

When he doesn't open his mouth to mine during another attempt, I pull back. "Do they kiss here?"

His hungry eyes are on my lips. I lick them and his growl vibrates in his chest. His own forked tongue flashes out to scent the air, reminding me of a snake. The sexiest snake I've ever seen. And just as dangerous and thrilling. "I have overheard Breccan and Aria talking about kiss."

"Kissing," I correct gently. I've never wanted something so much in my life. How would that tongue feel with mine? I want to know.

"Kissing," he repeats slowly. "What does it mean?"

I scoot over on the exam table as he perches by my side. Focusing on answering the question helps distract me from jumping him any more than I already have. If I had blood left in my face to blush, it'd be beet red. "Well, you press your lips together like we were. Sometimes, you open your mouths and rub your tongues together." I pause, considering my words. "It doesn't sound as attractive as it is, but it's much more pleasant while you're actually doing it."

His forked tongue flicks out again. My stomach seizes. "What is the purpose of this kissing?" he asks. When he speaks, he lifts one sharply nailed claw to scrap against my lower lip. Considering his job, it makes me wonder if he views everything with such an intense curiosity. It should make me feel like a test subject, but it's flattering. Where else would he direct his studious nature? The possibilities are more intriguing than I want to admit.

Too intriguing.

My breath freezes in my chest and I pull away when he leans forward for another kiss.

He frowns. "Did I do it wrong?" he asks. "Are you feeling ill?"

"No, I'm sorry. You didn't do anything wrong at all. In fact, you're doing everything so, so right."

I press a hand to my head where common sense wars with my excitement. It was my bad decisions on my part in the past that led me to this foreign planet in the first place. Despite how attracted I am to Calix and how much I want a repeat of his hands on me, I can't forget that he's a stranger...and my only hope at surviving.

"Then why do you wilt, my lilapetal?" His claws tangle in my hair, the ends lightly massaging my scalp, soothing the brewing headache beneath.

My eyes flutter closed. Starved for touch for so long makes being sensible almost impossible, especially when it comes to Calix, apparently. Gooseflesh erupts on my arms and I shiver. Calix, who never seems to miss anything, lifts my arm for closer inspection. His claws retract and the bumpy, thick pads of his over-large fingers trail gently down my skin. I can practically hear the gears in his brain turning. His intelligence is almost as attractive as the man himself.

The sensation overwhelms me. Heats my blood and makes me want to purr underneath his touch. I grip his hand to stop him. I want to explain, but the words make my tongue thick and my brain slow, so I stumble over my clarification. "You—I—this was nice. So nice you can't even imagine. But we should probably take this, us, slow so neither of us gets hurt."

Calix looks down at his hands. "Did I injure you? Sometimes we morts do not know our own strength."

Baffled, I study his face. Realization hits and I take his hands in my own. "Of course not. It's a human expression. It means I don't want either of us to make a mistake. This is all so new. I enjoyed what happened very much—"

"Then why not do it again?" he asks. "I want to help you, lilapetal, in all ways. Heal your body. Learn about your past. Kiss every inch of your skin."

I flush. For someone who doesn't understand kissing, he certainly has no problem with seduction. "Because we don't know each other," is all I can say, and even that tastes like a lie on my tongue.

"Our bodies know all there is to know, but I have observed Aria and Breccan enough to realize humans require more courting—more words—to be certain of a mate. Your voice is sweet to my ears, Emery-mine. I will listen to whatever you want to tell me. Come, we will get more comfortable."

He helps me down from the table and leads me to a sitting area on the other side of the labs. Grabbing an extra lab coat, which is slung over the back of a well-worn chair constructed of some sort of leather or hide, he helps cover me as I trade the sheet for the lab coat. The ancient couch to its right has faded so much the original color is indiscernible. When we sit on it, the cushions give underneath, causing me to lean into his side. Based on his self-satisfied grin, I know that is exactly his plan.

His fingers lift to the pulse hammering at my throat and he hums in approval. These aliens are sure a touchy-feely bunch if his actions are anything to judge by. Which reminds me... "If you want to know more about me, then I want to know more about you." I lift a brow. "Fair's fair."

He fits me into his side, half-lying against his body. It's been a long day and I'm thoroughly exhausted, so I don't have the energy to put up much of a fight. Besides, his closeness soothes the ragged edges inside of me. Being near him is like my own shot of sedative. My breathing slows, my heart settles, and my muscles loosen.

"A trade. I will agree to this. You may go first," Calix says, his voice a rhythmic rumble in my ear where my head rests against his chest.

I bite my lip as I consider what to tell him first. There's so much of my past I'd be ashamed for him to know. So much that would destroy the pedestal he has me on. But if I'm going to consider staying here, with this new community, I have to be honest about who I am and where I came from.

"My life wasn't glamorous like Aria's. I wasn't anyone important or noteworthy. My family was poor and couldn't afford much, but we were as happy as we could be when I was growing up. Ordinary, but happy."

"You are anything but ordinary, lilapetal, but go on."

His words only make me more determined for him to see the real me. "My illness cost my mother money, which meant she had to work harder to pay for doctors, medications, therapies. She wasn't home often and I was an only child, so I spent a lot of time when I wasn't in the hospital on my own." And when she died, I was completely on my own, having to fend for myself at an early age.

"You were lonely."

"Sometimes," I admit in a whisper.

"You will never be lonely again," Calix states firmly. "You are a part of our faction now. We will always be here for you, to help you, guide you, and give you safety. I vow this to you."

Emotion swells in my throat and I blink back the

sting of tears. "Thank you," I say when I'm sure I won't embarrass myself by crying all over him. "Now your turn. Tell me something about Calix. I've heard Aria talk about the women in cryo. If you have options, why me?" I should ask about his past, ask about the planet I've found myself on, but I want to know. He seems so sure of himself, of his interest in me. Maybe it's selfish, but dammit, I deserve to be selfish.

Calix adjusts our position so we're both reclining on the couch, with my back against the back of it and our legs intertwined. He dwarfs me completely, but I like it. I feel safe and protected, but at the same time the ease I feel in his arms scares me.

What if I grow used to having such security and it's ripped away?

"I had not planned to choose a mate from the females when we first learned of your existence."

I tip my head back so I can see his face. "You didn't?"

"No. There are ten of us and only five women. I want a mate, of course. All morts yearn for a family of their own. We all want mortyoung. For a long time, I never thought it would be a possibility for any of us. After losing so many due to sickness, I had given up hope. When we found you, I was happy enough to have the possibility of more for one of my brothers. I was certain I would give up the opportunity if I was selected to breed with one of the females. Certain, until I saw the cryotubes. Until I saw you. Then I knew you were mine and I would do anything to keep you."

"But what if I'm not who you think I am?"

"I think you are kind and gentle. More beautiful than a Mortuus sunset. I think you are stronger than you give yourself credit for."

I sigh, because I want to be the woman he sees. "Is that why you're helping me? Because you want a mate? Babies?"

"I am helping you because it is who I am, what I do. I could not save my people from The Rades, but I will figure out how to fix your lungs. Then, I will show you that you are meant for me."

Back home we used to have a saying about seeing someone's soul in their eyes, but I'd never really given it any thought until I locked eyes with Calix. His are vastly different from any man I've ever known, but when I look into them, I feel more connected to him than I ever have to anyone else.

Despite my earlier hesitation, I find myself leaning closer, needing to become a part of him, one with him. I don't have words for the need that pulses through me, so I don't try to explain it.

"Kiss?" he asks, so close that our lips brush together.

I answer with a moan, which morphs into a screech as a mad banging begins at the door.

Calix leaps to his feet, his teeth bared and claws extended.

"What's happening?" I ask, my chest tightening with an all too familiar anxiety.

It was only a matter of time.

When I stole her away, I knew they would come for us. What I did was against the rules. But I followed the rules. At first. I foolishly followed them for many solars, hoping against all odds that Emery would pull out of her poor health all on her own. Avrell had plenty of opportunity to heal her if it was within his abilities.

He didn't.

She lay there, her breath rattling in her chest, pleading for me to save her.

So that is what I am rekking doing.

*Bangbangbangbangbang!*

"Open up, you piece of rogshite!"

Emery's terror filled eyes widen. "W-What do they

w-want?" Her dulled teeth chatter away and I cock my nog to the side. It is rather unnerving, but I recall reading in Breccan's notes about this clattering noise in the sub-faction alien book that Sayer started in an effort to help us all understand them better. It is not a battle cry or a defense mechanism. It merely means they are cold.

I storm over to a closet and pull out a blanket that is much thicker than the warming sheet. Once I have wrapped it around her, I give her shoulder a reassuring squeeze before making my way over to the door. I am not one to keep my door closed, but when I brought Emery in, I closed it behind me. It is preprogrammed with a code they will never break. The only way those morts are getting in here is if I let them—which I will not—or if they force their way through.

"Let me in," Hadrian growls.

The youngest mort in our faction thinks that now that he is Aria's hand and protection when Breccan is unavailable, that he is the fiercest mort here.

I will tell you what is fierce.

When an empty-nog runt tries to interfere with the healing of *my* mate.

I will show him rekking fierce.

"No," I bark out, watching him through the small window. "I am searching for a cure."

He looks past me. "When Aria finds out, she will be furious."

"It is Aria's fault she is dying," I snarl.

His eyes widen. "The commander will not be pleased."

"I realized that risk before I took her."

He slams the door with his fist and storms off. I make my way over to a table near the bed and pull a freshly sanitized needle from the tray. Her eyes are drooping with drowsiness. It sends alarm racing down my spine, making my sub-bones crack along the way. I quickly attach a tube to the end of the syringe and then kneel in front of her.

"It will only feel like a pinch," I assure her. "I am going to draw some blood so I may test it."

She gives me a sleepy nod. Once I have taken the blood and bandaged her up, I drag over the oxygenating machine. This machine delivers air for longer periods than the simple breathing apparatus. Her hands swat at me, but I am firm with her. The rattling in her chest is ever-present and I want to make sure she does not suffocate. I put the mask around her nog and affix it so it stays in place.

"Rest, lilapetal," I urge, running my fingers through her silky tresses. "Let me work so I may try and help you."

Her eyes shine with thankfulness and then she flutters her lids closed. I get right to work creating different tests from her blood sample so I may look at them under the micro-viewer. I would like to test some of our older medicines that the microbots long took over in hopes to maybe find something we have over-looked. Perhaps the microbot technology is too advanced for the humans' bodies. As I work, my mind drifts to when I was a young mortling, playing in my father's office.

*"Sector 1779," Father says to his apprentice, Lox. "We need to take him to Sector 1779." Then, Father begins packing his bag with his supplies and work essentials.*

*"Sector 1779?" Lox asks.*

*I look up from the glass bottles I had been pretending to fill with magical medicines to heal my imaginary ailments. "What is Sector 1779, Father?"*

*"Not a place for young mortlings," he says. He turns to Lox and pulls off his glasses to rub at his eyes. Father works so hard and is always so tired. "Lox, ready the patient. We will take him to Sector 1779. They are the only facility with a surgical bot."*

*"Surgical bots are outdated technology, sir," Lox argues.*

*"Not everything gets better with newer technology,"*

*Father tells him. "The microbots do what they are programmed to do. But if they don't know what they are supposed to do, then they cannot do it."*

*"I don't understand," Lox mutters.*

*"It means I need to do it myself. I will man the surgical bot and do exploratory surgery. It is the only way."*

*"Sir!" Lox cries out. "Such procedures have been forbidden for years!"*

*My father clasps his hand on Lox's shoulder. "Our patient will die unless we figure out another way. Pack our things and ready the patient. We will leave at nightfall."*

*"Where is Sector 1779?" I ask.*

*Father walks over to me and ruffles my hair. "It is about three solars' worth of a treacherous journey across The Graveyard to the other side of Bleex Mountain. Too far for a youngster like you to travel. Perhaps when you are older, I will take you there to show you the dusty old surgical rooms. It has long been abandoned, but certainly not forgotten."*

A banging on the door startles me from my work. When I drag my eyes from the micro-viewer and my sample, I see Commander Breccan glaring at me from the other side of the glass.

Rekk.

Ignoring him, I tweak the magnifiers by 1000 to study the biological code of her blood cells. I do not find anything right away and my intuition tells me it is not so simple as finding a deformity in her blood cells and reprogramming the microbots. I wanted to rule it out nonetheless.

With a sigh, I run some more tests on her blood, until I hear an obnoxious clanking. Jerking my attention to the door, I am annoyed to see Oz. If Oz is here, that means Breccan is going to have our faction's mechanic try to dismantle the door.

I do not need this distraction.

"Good solar, Calix," Uvie chirps, despite my manual override to shut her down. I open my mouth to tell her silent mode again, but Sayer's familiar voice takes over. "What the rekk are you doing, Calix?"

"What I have to," I grumble. "Silent mode."

He chuckles, his voice echoing over the speakers. "You can't silence me, you piece of rogshite."

"Then go away. I am working."

"Breccan is not happy with you," Sayer tells me, as if I do not already know this.

"I am aware," I snap back. "Silent mode."

It goes quiet for a moment, and I let out a breath of relief that maybe I have gotten him to go away for at least the time being.

Rolling away in my chair, I slide over to my cabinet with my father's old notes. I pull open a drawer and start thumbing through the files. I hunt for Sector 1779, but nothing is labeled by that name. Closing my eyes, I try to remember any details about the patient that sent him that way. What was his name? What was he ailing from?

Belin.

It comes to me just like that and I quickly locate Belin's file. Once I flip it open, I find mountains of notes. Belin, twenty-two revolutions old, suffered from an adverse reaction to a sticky fernus. The plant, when in contact with, emits a pink powder. If ingested or breathed in, the powder changes its molecular structure, turning into a sticky paste. Galen has managed to create a substance from its powder that we use when patching our equipment, facility windows and cracks, and our minnasuits. He removes the harmful toxins in the powder form by sifting out the tiny pink crystals and then turns it into the paste. But in the past, before modern technology, the sticky fernus was a problem for Belin. My father took him away to Sector 1779, the mort struggling for air and on his deathbed, and when they came back, Belin was a new man.

A sawing—metal against metal—jerks me from my

thoughts. Emery wakes from her nap and stares at me with confusion in her eyes.

"I need more time," I grumble, running my fingers through my short, unruly hair and tugging.

"You don't have much of it," Sayer tells me out of thin air, making Emery jolt in surprise.

"It is just Sayer," I assure her. "He is trying to... actually, I am unsure what it is he is trying to do aside from annoy me out of my rekking nog."

"Good solar, Emery," Sayer greets her.

"Eh, hello," she whispers back.

"Are you well?" he inquires. "Calix isn't hurting you?"

"Mortarekk—"

She cuts me off as she replies sharply. "I am fine. Leave us be."

"Very well," he says with a sigh and then says no more.

She reaches out her hand and I abandon my chair to prowl over to her. I kneel beside her and hold her cold, weak hand in mine. Tears well in her pretty blue eyes—tears I want to lick away. Instead, I watch them cascade down her pale cheeks. I pull her palm to my cheek to warm it against my flesh.

"I don't want them to get in," she rasps through her mask.

I turn and inhale her scent from her hand. "I will do everything in my power to keep them out until I can heal you."

More tears roll from her eyes. "This isn't something that can be healed in a few hours, Calix. I'm not sure it can ever be healed." She makes a sad, choked sound. "I can feel it. I'm going to die here."

A growl rumbles through me and I shake my nog. "You will not die," I assure her even though my words sound like lies. "I will not let you."

Her fingertips flutter against my cheekbone. "It's not your choice. There was a design—by a higher being —and I'm being erased from it."

I do not understand her words, but I feel them in my bones. I do not like them. So final and sure. As though she does not think she belongs breathing the same air as everyone else. As though her time was always limited.

I'll give her all the time I can, even if it is the last thing I do.

I can hear Breccan calling to me over Oz's work, but I ignore him. My focus is on healing her and keeping her comfortable. Releasing her, I make my way over to the refrigeration unit. Often, when immersed in work, I will stay locked away and never make it to the nutrition bay. I keep some rations here for those times. Pulling out a bowl of dried vin-fruit—a sweet delicacy we were rewarded on one of Galen's most recent successful harvests—I make my way back over to Emery. The morsels are round and wrinkly. The vin-fruit was fascinating to watch grow in the lab. Vines overgrew the containers they were planted in and tiny balls filled with orange-colored juice grew all over. They are bitter eaten right from the vine, but when you pluck them and let them dry out, they wrinkle up and become sweet. Galen claims they are packed with important nutrients, but they taste too lovely to be good for you. His bitter green bunches certainly are not tasty and they are incredibly nutritious.

"Eat," I instruct, resting the bowl beside Emery. I pull away the oxygen mask to let it hang around her neck and pluck a vin-fruit from the bowl. Obediently, she parts her bluish plump lips and accepts the nutrients I'm offering.

"I like these," she says, a smile ghosting her lips. "Great idea for a last meal."

I scowl at her. "It is the first of many."

Her eyes grow soft at my words. "Thank you for trying."

I nod my nog at her and offer her more morsels. She eats them all and then eyes the bowl with longing.

"I will procure more later. For now, get some rest," I say as I pull the mask back over her mouth and nose.

She frowns. "What will you eat?"

"I am not hungry. My studies await me."

I start to pull away, but she takes my hand. Her hand squeezes mine tightly. We share a long stare before I reluctantly pull away from her. The sawing outside the door has intensified. I rise to my feet and stalk over to where they're working.

"Go away," I bark at them.

Commander bares his double fangs at me. "Open the rekking door, Calix."

"Let me work in peace. I am trying to help her," I bite out.

With a door between us, it is easy to not cower under his domineering glare. Perhaps the desire to protect my mate overshadows all senses.

"We can help her together. Locking her away solves nothing," he says, his voice not as harsh.

"She is frightened of you all."

"That is why she belongs with Aria for the time being." His eyes drift past me. "Have you...touched her?"

I think about the way she felt as I brought her pleasure. Her taste. Her sounds. Her scent. "She is safe

55

with me," I growl, ignoring his question. "Leave us be. She chooses to be with me."

His eyes widen slightly before a scowl takes over. "I make those choices," he grunts. "I am the commander and you need to remember your place. What you are doing is grounds for punishment. There is a reform cell with your name on it if you do not open this door now."

"I am sorry," I say as I retreat from the window. "I cannot obey, Commander. Not when my lilapetal's life hangs in the balance."

I don't wait for his response and settle back in my chair.

"I get what you're trying to do," Sayer says again, making his irritating presence known. "I respect that. Just know that Aria doesn't approve, therefore Breccan doesn't either. It's in your best interest to open that door."

"And it is in your best interest to go the rekk into silent mode."

The piece of rogshite laughs at me before going silent once more, giving me a chance to look at my father's notes.

The notes are detailed. So many notes. Greedily, I read over every question in the margin. Every calcula-tion. It is evident from the notes and the drawings, that

Lox and my father took Belin to Sector 1779 right away. The traveling to Bleex Mountain was treacherous, but they eventually managed to get around it and to the building. It took some searching, but they prepped one of the old surgical rooms and booted up a surgical bot. Father explained how he had to clean and sterilize everything, including the patient. He and Lox wore protective clothing and they used something called Haxinth—a detailed formula he notated—to administer to Belin to make him what Father called a "living corpse." Belin, under the influence of Haxinth, became unfeeling and unaware of pain. He said it was imperative that Belin not be awake and with his senses during the exploratory surgery.

Lox stood by Belin while Father sat in the desk with the controls. The surgical bot was mounted on the ceiling and Father controlled it from across the room. His notes said the bot was more precise than a mort's hand. Together with the surgical bot, Lox and my father cut open the "living corpse" and made incisions in his lungs. With a tool attached to the bot's "hand," Father was able to soak up the sticky fern secretions that clung to the mort's lungs. According to his notes, so much time passed that they were starved and dizzy, yet they kept going until they had cleaned out every bit of it. Father used the machine and some microbots to close the incisions and then the larger one on his chest.

Belin must have reacted to the Haxinth badly at first, though, because they could not rouse him for many solars. His wound from the surgery healed, but he remained lifeless, although no longer needing respiratory assistance. My father and Lox traded shifts watching over him. Talking to him. Injecting him with nutrients and different medicines in hopes that something would wake him. On the twelfth solar, Belin woke. His voice was scratchy and raw, but he was able to sit up. They had healed him.

My mind whirs at the possibilities. What if Sector 1779 holds the key to Emery's health and survival? What if I can heal her like my father healed Belin?

I am jolted from all thoughts when the door is smashed open and a very angry commander storms in with several equally infuriated morts at his back.

"I tried to warn you," Sayer mumbles from above me through the comms system.

"Get out!" I roar at Breccan, standing from my seat and taking a protective stance in front of Emery.

Commander shakes his nog in disappointment. "Draven, I want him bound and taken to a reform cell."

Before I can fight, Draven pushes past Breccan

and pounces on me. The mort is half crazed and stronger than a sabrevipe. He shoves me against some shelves, sending precious instruments crashing to the ground, and jerks my arms behind me. I am cuffed with a zuta-metal clamp and unable to move a muscle.

"Calix," Emery whimpers from behind the mask, her blue eyes alight with fear.

I struggle against Draven's hold to no avail. "This is not over," I vow to her. "I will find out how to heal you. Stay alive for me."

Breccan tries to comfort her and she scrambles from his touch. It makes me blind with rage, forcing me to charge at my commander to protect her. Using just my shoulder, I shove him away from her and tackle him to the floor. My fangs are bared and gnashing near the vein in his throat, desperate to make purchase. Before I can tear out the pulsating vein with my teeth, I am jerked away. Avrell walks in with a syringe dripping with something.

"No!"

His eyes are apologetic as he pushes the needle into my arm. Everything goes black almost instantly. The last thing I see is a flash of yellow hair and wide, panicked blue eyes before I am thrust into nothingness.

[ 5 ]

EMERY

BEING TORN AWAY from Calix is even worse than when I woke up in a strange world surrounded by even stranger beings. If I'd had a doubt about my fate, it's erased as the commander called Breccan wraps his powerful arms around me to keep me from struggling free. Not that I have the energy to do so.

"Calm yourself, young one. My apologies for Calix's behavior. Isolating you like this was reprehensible and he will be dealt with accordingly." The words are meant to be reassuring, but they merely cause my chest to tighten even more.

I struggle for breath. When I speak, the words are faint and wheezy. "I asked him to," I tell him between heaving breaths. "He was helping me. He didn't do anything wrong. Please don't hurt him."

My vision contracts to a pinpoint and at the center is the stern face of the commander. I don't know how Aria puts up with him. Unlike Calix, who is always so comforting, calm, and composed, this alien's expression is uncompromising and stern. My already racing heart thumps double-time in my chest. Standing up to this beast of a man is a testament to how much Calix has already affected me. I've never stood up for myself before.

As my lungs struggle to work, I nearly laugh at myself. The one time I've shown defiance may be my last.

"We're not going to hurt him," comes Aria's voice from behind me. "If I've learned anything from Breccan and my own actions it's that we can't let one person's motives or impulsiveness go unchecked for the sake of the whole faction. Breccan is a fair leader and Calix will be fine. For now, we are taking you to the medical bay where Avrell can make sure you're safe and healthy."

I fight in Breccan's hold at the thought of what they may do to Calix. "Tell him to put me down," I demand to Aria as she comes into my line of sight. My face flushes with heat, both because I'm embarrassed my orders come out as a squeak and from anger that my body fails me even now when it's so important.

Aria sends me a pitying glance, which only makes me angrier. At least Calix didn't look at me with that sort of fake sympathy. He is the only one here who cares about me and they took him away and are treating me like less than human.

"We're almost there," Aria says.

"I said put me down!" The shout burns through my throat and doesn't help the tightness in my chest. Anxiety can worsen asthma attacks. Getting worked up won't help anything, but if I'm going to die here in this strange place, I want the one person who cares about me to be with me. Frustrated tears leak from my eyes and I knuckle them away with a bruising swipe.

"No," Breccan interrupts Aria's response. "You are ill and aren't making any sense. We will get you to Avrell where you will be safe and you're going to stop this nonsense before you hurt yourself."

My voice is little more than a croak now. "You may be the leader here, but I deserve to have a say in how I'm treated. That's my right. If I want to refuse treatment, you should respect that."

Breccan's gait doesn't change, nor does his expression. "Each life on Mortuus is precious. I will not risk anyone's safety, not even yours and not even if it goes against your wishes."

Outraged, my head jerks toward Aria as we pause

at another door. "How can you let him treat me like this?"

Aria bites her lip, then says, "We really are just trying to help, Emery. The morts here can be a bit impulsive, especially when it comes to someone they consider a mate."

I glare at her, then turn to face Avrell, who I remember vaguely from when I was removed from the pod. Unlike Breccan's wild mane of hair, Avrell's is carefully shorn, almost preppy. When he smiles, I note his fangs have been filed down. It gives him a kind, approachable appearance. If I weren't so absolutely steamed, it would have been welcoming. Of all the aliens I've met so far aside from Calix, Avrell is the one I'd be most comfortable with.

His face visibly softens in relief when Breccan places me on an examination table in front of him. "I've been ever so worried about you," Avrell says as he begins to hook me up to monitors. I almost expect a sizzle of heat to pass from his fingers to my skin like when Calix did the same thing, but Avrell's touch is competent and clinical.

"How is she?" Breccan asks and I grit my teeth at being discussed like I'm invisible.

"Her heart rate is high and her lungs are working overtime even though her blood-oxygen level is low."

With a sympathetic glance at me, he adds, "She's having a very hard time breathing. I'm surprised she hasn't lost consciousness."

"Is there anything you can do?" Aria asks. I don't look at her. She was supposed to be my friend, but her actions leave me feeling betrayed, alone. Without Calix, I'm bereft.

To me, Avrell says, "I'm going to administer a light sedative to help calm your nerves. It will hopefully alleviate the stress on your lungs and allow you to breathe more normally." He preps my arm and inserts a small needle. I barely even feel the pinch. "It'll take a few moments to take effect."

I close my eyes and imagine he's Calix, which allows me to relax in small increments. If I'm going to die, I don't want it to be while I'm surrounded by these strangers. I must get well enough to find out where they're keeping Calix so I can see him again, if only for a short while.

———

WHEN I WAKE AGAIN, the room is empty. The only sound is the dull, monotonous drone from the computer as it reads my vital signs. The ache in my chest is still there, but much less pronounced.

I push to a sitting position and groan. Now that I'm not panicking and can somewhat breathe, all the other aches and pains my body is experiencing make themselves known. My head hurts, my stomach aches, and I could use a week's worth of uninterrupted sleep. Despite it all, my first priority is finding Calix.

Swinging my legs over the side of the examination table, I get to my wobbly feet, dragging their monitors behind me. The room is about the size of a regular bedroom, with one door leading into what looks like an office, and another automated door that empties out into the hallway. I can't access the hall door without one of those bracelets the commander had been wearing around his wrist.

"Good solar, alien Emery," Uvie chirps in greeting. "How may I assist you?"

Of course it wouldn't be that easy.

"Silent mode," I order, remembering how Calix had used the command before. I'm shocked when she goes silent.

My stomach cramps and I double over. Much as I want to plot my escape to find Calix, it won't do me any good if I don't have the energy to make it to him. A quick search through the bay of cabinets near the exam table turns up more of the fruit Calix had given me before. I choke down a couple—their taste is no longer sweet on my tongue while I'm flooded with worry—then wash it back with a cup of water I retrieve from the sink.

I leave the empty container and the dripping cup on the counter, my attention turning to the office door. As I pushed through, thankful it's unlocked and empty, I give a silent apology to Avrell for invading his privacy. Computers and strange medical contraptions buzz and whirl, but what interests me the most is the map on the wall opposite his desk.

Leaning forward to study the layout more closely, I can't hear anything over the rush of blood in my ears. If I can find out where they're keeping him, the reform cell Breccan had called it, then I can save him like he'd saved me.

"What are you doing?" comes a voice from behind me.

I screech and whirl around, my hand clutching at my racing heart to find Avrell leaning against the door, his pointed ears flicking. His lips are pulled back in a wan smile that bares his filed down teeth.

"Avrell, I-I'm just—"

"Trying to find a way to escape?" he finishes.

My stomach twists. "No, I was trying to find out where you're keeping Calix." Might as well be honest. I've already been caught.

Avrell gestures for me. "Let's get you back to the bed. You need to rest."

He tries to take my hand, but I pull away from him. "No, I don't want to rest anymore. I want to know what you're doing with Calix. He was only trying to help me. I'm not going to comply with any of your tests until you let me see him." My voice rises with each word until the end when my words echo off the small room.

"What's going on in here?" Aria says as she comes around the corner to Avrell's side. Breccan, to my growing disappointment, follows close behind.

"What are you doing out of bed?" Breccan practically growls.

"She wants to see Calix," Avrell informs them.

Aria is already shaking her head. "No, sweetheart, you need to rest and let Avrell figure out what's going on. Trust me, he's a good doctor. He'll take good care of you."

"I already had a good doctor. I want him back. Like I told Avrell, I'm not going to follow any of your directions. I'll fight you every step of the way, unless you let me see Calix."

Breccan, who'd been uncharacteristically silent, lifts a hand when Avrell and Aria open their mouths to argue. "Listen, little one, I understand you want to see your mate, but Calix has broken the rules."

My mate?

The thought isn't a horrible one, but I pack that thought away for another time.

"It's not safe for any mort to follow their whims as they see fit," he explains. "Doing so could put our entire population at risk if something were to go amiss. Including yourself and the other aliens."

I'd barely given any thought to the other women on board, or the other morts for that matter. "Calix only wanted to help me and he has. He's been trying hard to figure out what's wrong with me. If you truly value my life, you'll bring him back."

The three of them share a look and Breccan says, "We can't let his transgression go unpunished."

"So you're punishing me, too?" I hiss.

"Of course not," Aria interjects. "You're free here, you're safe with us."

"If I haven't done anything wrong then there's no reason for you to keep me locked up here like an animal in a zoo. I'm feeling much better now and we'll all figure out what's wrong with me much faster if you take me to Calix, otherwise we can keep going round and round and nothing is going to get accomplished."

Aria puts a hand on Breccan's arm and he says, "I do not like being backed into a corner." His black eyes pin me to the spot, then he says, "But I can't help but respect you for fighting hard for your mate. I too, have experienced this. I will take you to Calix, but he is not to be released until the following solar, is that understood?"

The bands in my chest loosen, but I keep my spine stiff. I don't want Breccan to see me as weak. I don't want any of them to. "Then take me to him."

## [ 6 ]
## CALIX

Cold.

Every part of me is numb.

Am I in The Eternals?

A thundering inside my nog reminds me I am not dead. That I am as alive as the solar I was born. But I have lost my senses and they are slowly returning back. My heart is erratically beating inside my chest cavity, as though it is trying to escape.

Why would my heart want to escape?

Blue eyes. Yellow hair. Pale and soft and dying.

"Emery," I croak, blinking my eyes open against the darkness.

A bulb flickers and hums from the hallway. It takes a moment to realize I am lying on a cot inside a reform cell. Cold and alone.

Rekk.

Whatever Avrell injected me with slows me down. My mind begs for me to rise to my feet and rage. To tear the metal bars from the walls and make my escape. But I am weak and weary. Frustration seeps inside my bones.

I need to get to her.

Before it is too late.

"She's not there," Sayer's voice rumbles from a speaker nearby.

"This really is punishment," I complain. "Having you follow me everywhere I go, echoing all my thoughts."

"Just thought you might need a little company," he says in his jovial way that normally does not bother me, but gets under my skin this solar.

"Silent mode. Ever heard that command?"

He laughs and then it goes silent again.

Thank the rekking orbs. I need to think, and I cannot do that with Sayer invading my mind.

Sitting up, I study the small cell. A urinal sits in the corner beside a sink. The cell is empty. Not often do we have to bring anyone down here. Last mort down here was Draven. When he had been lost to The Rades' madness. I had watched him from the feed as Breccan cared for him. We were all sure he would have died. Somehow, despite how the disease ravaged him, he lived.

She will live too.

Our people are stubborn and will fight for the ones we care about, even when they are too weak to fight for themselves.

Something clanks nearby and then I hear foot-steps. Then, Emery comes into view, wearing a loose-fitting minnasuit and boots. I am so surprised to see her, I almost wonder if I am imagining it. I find a way to get my legs to work and shakily make my way over to the door. She rushes over to me, her chest rattling loudly.

"Calix," she says, choking on a sob as she reaches through the bars to get to me.

I walk into her embrace and hug her back. My nose finds her hair and I inhale her sweet scent. Now that she is back in my arms, I do not want to let her go.

My eyes lift to find Breccan glowering at me, a folder tucked against his chest in his arm. Aria, also frowning, stands beside him. They both regard me with disappointment.

"I need to get out of here," I bark at him. "I need to find a way to heal her."

Breccan shakes his nog. "Not for at least one more

solar. You are still burning with rage. You are unpredictable, Calix. I am sorry."

A growl rumbles from me. "We do not...we do not have time for this."

"I understand, which is why Avrell will be assisting. I will bring you your tablet and I have brought what you were reading. But for now, she stays out here and you stay in there."

Emery pulls away from me and storms over to Breccan. She yanks the folder from his grip and hisses at him, "Leave. You both have done nothing but make things worse."

Aria gapes at her while Breccan's brows furrow deeper.

"Very well," Aria says softly. "If you need us, you know where we'll be."

As soon as they're gone, Emery's teary eyes meet mine as she hands me the folder. "I hate it here."

I wince at her words. "I am sorry."

She shakes her nog, sending two tears snaking down her cheeks. "Not you. Them. This place. Our predicament. I wish we had met someplace else. Where I had my medicine and we were free to just be together without anyone bothered by it."

Reaching through the bars, I swipe away her tears with my thumbs, my claws gently sliding across her pale flesh. "We are alone now. We will figure out a way. Things will get better. I swear this to you, lilapetal."

She smiles and hands me the folder. "I trust you. Until you're free, tell me what you need and I'll fetch it. Firstly, tell me where to find some blankets. It's cold down here."

Sayer makes his presence known once more. "Third door on your right, Emery," he instructs. "I'm here if you need me."

For once, his voice is welcome.

---

"Rogshite," I mutter under my breath.

Emery sits up and leans her nog to peer inside my cell. We are sitting back to back against the bars. I am studying my father's notes while she taps away on my tablet to pass the time.

"What is it?" she murmurs. "Everything okay?"

"It is just this..." I point at the messy scrawling left by my father. "The surgical bot. After Belin fell ill after being exposed to one of our toxic plants, he used this machine. Using this technology, he was able to cut him open and explore inside his body to remove the tarry substance. They tracked his progress all the way over here at this facility via a comms system. Belin underwent these treatments where a certain medicine was breathed into him."

She widens her glassy blue eyes. "Do you not have the medicine here?"

"No," I grunt. "From his notes, he said that microbots were the future. That this technology was outdated. The morts moved here many revolutions ago. But..."

I think about the rough, harsh terrain and climate that stands between us and those machines. The Graveyard. Sabrevipes. Geostorms. Pathogens.

"No," I growl. "It is rekking impossible."

"What is?" She reaches through the bars and threads her fingers with mine.

I bring her hand to my nose and inhale her sweet, addictive scent. "If the technology is still there, we could try it. Even without that medicine. I could give the formula for Haxinth to Avrell. He could make some for us to use for the procedure. Then, once inside, I could directly examine the issues and maybe the microbots would do their job if applied straight to the source."

She grins at me. "Let's go. Let's do it. Anything to get out of this place."

I squeeze her hand. "Emery, it is not that easy. In

fact, it is nearly an impossible journey. At least three treacherous solars' worth of travel through The Grave-yard. So many awful things could happen along the way. I do not want to lose you on a chance."

She leans in, her hot breath close to my face. "This is my only chance. I don't think you realize that. Nothing here works. If there's a machine that you think could help, we have to take that chance."

Pressing my face against the bar, I seek out her sweet lips. She kisses me softly. I want to pull her in here with me and mate with her properly. Show her how much my soul has bound itself to hers. The stars created this union and I will be rekking damned if they try and tear it apart.

"We will have to vanish," I whisper in case Sayer is listening. "While no one is looking." I motion for the tablet. "I will make a list and where everything is at that we will need. Just be quiet and nobody will notice. If you need to take breaks, do it. I need you as strong as you can be for this journey."

Her eyes glitter with excitement. "We're really going to do this?"

"Together."

She kisses me again, this time, her tongue eagerly plunging into my mouth to dance with mine. We almost attempted it before, and now we are finally doing it. For a moment, I am dizzied by her immensely sweet taste. Like her tears, but even sweeter if possible. Now I understand why Breccan devours Aria so often. These aliens taste rekking delicious.

"Thank you," she murmurs when she finally pulls away.

All I can do is grin at her, my forked tongue flicking out on my bottom lip to savor the last of her.

---

I'M SHOWING Emery what one of our weapons does when we hear footsteps. Quick and fierce.

"Hide this bag," I growl in warning.

Before she can get it put away, Breccan and Draven round the corner. Emery reaches beyond the bars to grab my hand as though she is afraid of being torn from me again. A growl rumbles from my throat.

Breccan glowers at me. "Your constant disrespect for authority is alarming, Calix."

"You, of all morts, should understand," I snarl.

Draven's brows lift and he smirks at me.

Breccan, thankfully, relents. "I do understand, which is why I have not throttled your brainless rekking nog." His sharp stare roams over the space and he eyes the bag. "Going somewhere?"

I rise to my feet and point to the lock. "Let me out."

Breccan's jaw clenches. His sub-bones pop in his neck, but I ignore the sound that usually intimidates me into submission. Not this solar. This solar, I am filled with the fire to protect my mate. "A geostorm is coming. Big one."

The fire is snuffed and I deflate.

"Then we must hurry," Emery whispers, tugging at my minnasuit.

"Hurry for what?" Breccan asks as he edges closer. Draven holds back, near the door. He always has an escape at the ready. "Were you two planning on leaving?" His eyes are wide in astonishment.

"With good reason," I try to explain. "My father worked over at Sector 1779 on the outdated equipment. I am sure it could be of use to Emery."

I expect backlash and argument. Not a nod of agreement.

"I will have Draven and Oz prepare one of the terrainsters. You and Emery should get with Aria and Avrell to pack the other necessities for your travels. But you must be swift if you intend on beating the geostorm," Breccan says as he pulls an old-fashioned metal key from his pocket.

He unlocks the door and I yank it open to get to

K WEBSTER & NICOLE BLANCHARD

Emery. The moment she is really in my arms, I can relax. Breccan smiles at me and Draven's black eyes flare with something akin to disgust, as though touching her is horrible and repulsive. She is anything but. She is perfect, and she is mine.

"Why the sudden change of heart?" I demand.

Breccan scrubs his face with his palm, his claws dangerously close to carving out his eyeball. "We need information." Then a sigh. "Just like you. Information we did not bring here because it was no longer useful. Our people—the females—were dying out." His jaw clenches. "Avrell says they used to have a nursery inside Sector 1779. If anything goes wrong with my mortyoung, we need to have every bit of information within our claws. The terrainster is big enough to carry some equipment back."

"We'll make several trips and bring back as much as we can," I agree without hesitation. One solar, I hope for Emery to carry my own mortyoung. And I want them both to be safe and healthy.

Breccan frowns. "This geostorm is gearing up to be one of the worst in our history. Potentially cataclysmic. I'll have all morts here hunting and gathering. We're going to fortify the facility against it. According to the reports, you have around four solars to safely get there and prepare yourselves against it. We'll remain in contact."

"When will the storm pass?" I ask, hating the dread pooling inside me.

"Our best guess is over two hundred solars."

Sayer chimes in above us. "Give or take. Galen and I have been watching the geostorm and it keeps changing course. This one is unpredictable, but two hundred solars is our best guess based on its size and movement."

"Two hundred solars," I hiss in confusion.

"We can only hope it is enough time...before..." Breccan's jaw clenches and he looks away. "I cannot lose Aria or my son."

Son?

"We will be back in time," I vow to my commander, who has finally gifted what I need. "Everything is going to work out."

Emery squeezes me. Even she believes my words.

I rekking hope I can stay true to them.

## [ 7 ]
### EMERY

I HAVE to leave Calix to go with Aria to the sub-faction where empty rooms wait for the other women still in cryosleep. She leads me to a big observation area and keys in a command that opens the huge window in what she calls the common room.

The view on the other side causes me to stumble backward, even though I've seen it before. The vast, empty plains angry with red-orange dunes as far as the eye can see. In the distance, thick storm clouds blot out the horizon. Just before the clouds, looming like a malevolent shadow, are the mountains that could mean my salvation—or my death.

Was I an idiot for even attempting this? The facility here is safe, I know this for sure. Whatever awaits on the other side of those mountains? A total question mark. The sector Calix has read about in his father's notes could have been destroyed. I could be risking both our lives in this crazy endeavor.

"I know you hate me," Aria begins.

I look up from the minnasuit—one that's smaller and more form-fitting than the other—I'm trying to figure out how to fasten. "I don't hate you," I say before she can speak again. "I wish you'd let me make decisions for myself."

My response stuns her to silence and then she gives a little wry laugh. "You sound just like my little sister, Limerick. I used to boss her around, too. I guess when I realized Calix woke you up, I tried to be your big sister, too, rather than the friend I should have been." She pauses, rubbing a hand over the gentle swell of her belly. "I guess I was a little desperate for her and I took it out on you. Can you forgive me?"

Family.

The concept is a foreign one to me, that's for sure. It hadn't occurred to me she looked at me in that way. The only family I'd ever known—my mother—died when I was younger. I admit as much to her. "I lost my only family when I was a teenager. It's probably as much my fault as it is yours. I don't have much experience in the family department lately either."

Aria lifts her hand from her stomach and starts

forward like she might pull me in for a hug, but I side-step her attempt. Hurt flashes in her eyes, briefly, but she blinks it away. Maybe one day I'll feel comfortable with her, but I'm still harboring some hard feelings toward her and how she's handled things on my behalf.

"I hate that you're leaving just when we've started to work things out," Aria says with a small smile. "Promise me you won't do anything stupid while you're out there?"

I think of the mountains, the long, almost impossible trip, and the burning in my chest I'm trying to ignore. "I'll do my best," I tell her. "Do you know exactly how we're supposed to be traveling?"

She pulls me to the window. "That's what I was going to talk to you about before you left." Aria points to a dock of sorts outside the facility. "Calix requested you use one of the little four-wheeler like vehicles they have. They call them terrainsters. It's not in the best repair, but we can't afford to let the other go, not with the geostorm coming."

"I understand." Nerves jangle in the pit of my stomach, but I've committed to our plan now. There's no turning back.

"You'll be safe," Oz, the mort covered in grease, explains in an almost shy way. He squints his eyes and then smiles reassuringly. "I have tested it several times."

"Trust," Calix murmurs to me. "Oz can fix just about anything. Between him and Jareth, I know it will work just fine." He saunters over to the vehicle to toss in some gear.

The entire faction—the group of morts and us two human girls—stands on the ship deck, fully covered in what they call zu-gear over our minnasuits. Several morts, who are unrecognizable behind their masks, load items into the back of the vehicle we'll be taking.

"Remember," the one with slightly slanted eyes says. Galen, I think. "Don't eat any plants on your journey. They most likely aren't safe. The rations I prepared will be sufficient."

I nod my understanding.

The one named Jareth bounds over to me the moment Galen leaves. "Just push the button and watch the brilliance happen." He points at Oz. "Genius, that one." His lips turn up in a cocky way from behind his mask. "Of course, the vacuuroom wouldn't be possible without my knowledge of metals and their capabilities. You'll understand later."

I barely utter out my thanks before someone else is in my face.

"I'd take you for a ride in *Mayvina*," Theron, a guy just as energetic as Hadrian, says, "but she's a little ill at the moment. We're working on making her as good as new."

Another giant mort nudges me with his elbow. "Don't take rides from the likes of him," a familiar voice says. "Stick with Calix. He'll keep you safe." Sayer. I recognize his voice from many of the times he spoke over the comms.

"I trust him," I tell Sayer firmly.

He grins from behind his mask.

"Magnastrikes," someone growls from farther away, making me jump. My eyes lock with the wild ones of Draven. "They're explosive radiation strikes. You may encounter them near or within a geostorm." He mutters out a few more technical things about these terrifying things before backing away.

Before I know it, Calix is ushering me into the vehicle and Hadrian throws up what I now know are "rogcow horns," to bid us goodbye.

Definitely no turning back now.

I want to turn back.

Calix whips across the dunes in what I've not-so-lovingly named the dust-mobile. It cuts over the dunes of red-orange sand with ease, but leaves thick clouds of the stuff in its wake. The heat outside is a relentless onslaught and bakes me inside the tight-fitting minna-suit. I'm reminded back to the hazy lesson that Aria gave me not long after I'd awoken. The R-levels, they'd called them. Or radiation levels. Made worse by the intensity of the sun. Aria's face had darkened at the mention of how easily both humans and morts could burn from exposure.

If I thought it was hard to breathe inside the facility, it's almost impossible outside.

I can't tell that to Calix. The look of determination on his face behind his mask snaps my jaws together. I got us into this and I'll survive. For Calix, I'll do what I have to do to make it to the other side of that mountain.

"Do you travel outside the facility often?" I ask through our comms units that are located inside our helmets. The sound of wheezing between the words echoes back through my headset, but I ignore it and pray Calix will, too.

"No, unless it is required. I am of more use in the lab. It is rare a mort volunteers to go outside the facility because it can be so dangerous. The R-levels are a big problem," he explains. "And then, there are pathogens in the atmosphere that cause The Rades." The deadly disease he'd already mentioned that had wiped out most of their numbers some years ago.

My chest tightens. "You won't get it, will you?" Swamped with despair, I reach over and squeeze his thick, muscular thigh, hoping for some comfort in the touch. Selfish. You should have thought of this before you made him leave the safety of the facility.

"Do not fret. I have taken every precaution. As long as we wear our rebreathers under our masks when we travel, we will both be protected." He pats my hand reassuringly.

"How far away is Bleex Mountain?" The landscape is mostly obscured by the murky dust clouds that seem to hover a few feet above the dunes, but what I've seen is identical in every direction. I'm glad he's driving because we've only been traveling for a short time and I'm already lost.

"Three, maybe four solars' travel."

Sector 1779 is probably a pipe dream and I know that. If we survive the journey, it may be damaged beyond repair. The tools Calix believes are there could be destroyed or lost. For once in my life, I'm being selfish...I just hope it doesn't cost Calix his.

"Are you sure we can make it there safely?" I shift

in the seat, unable to get comfortable. It's not for lack of the dust-mobile, its seats are surprisingly nice.

"Worry not, lilapetal, I am not going to let anything happen to you."

I blow out a breath. I'm starting to annoy myself. "Remind me again how it will go. Just one more time." I'd had Calix explain the trip to me several times before we left, and several more once we got on the road.

"We will travel as much as we dare during the daylight hours. The weather conditions are too unfavorable at night to risk it. Then we will set up camp with our portable vacuuroom."

Even though Oz hinted at it and Jareth bragged about it, I still don't get it.

"Tell me more about the vacuuroom." I rest my head against his shoulder and wish I weren't wearing the helmet so I could inhale his comforting scent. I'll have to settle for the memory, at least until we camp for the night.

He humors me, explaining how the portable tent-like structure is a mini-version of the facility in the way that it has a decontamination area and impenetrable walls, which will allow us privacy and protection against the elements and predators as we travel. Aria already filled me in on the horrors of sabrevipes and I am in no hurry to run into one.

We travel for an eternity and I rest in fits. At first, I try to take in the wonder of the foreign landscape surrounding me, but the uniqueness only lasts so long when we're surrounded by barren, towering dunes and scraggly mountains as far as the eye can see.

The only reason I even considered risking this trip —the reason I haven't quite mustered the nerve to tell Calix, is the longer I'm on this planet, the less energy I seem to have. Even in the sterile environment of the facility, I struggled to breathe. There has to be a cure. There has to. I cling to that thought rather than wondering what it will be like to be alone with Calix in our little tent with nothing but time.

My mind drifts to the past.

After my mother died. Everything was so hard back then. It changed me. The things I had to do to preserve my life were what ended me up on that vessel in the first place. These guys saved me, unbeknownst to them. And no matter how awful this planet is, I have no intentions of ever leaving it.

Sooner or later, I'll have to tell him the truth. I just hope he can forgive me when I do.

Hours later, Calix slows the dust-mobile to a stop and I shake off the remnants of sleep. It doesn't seem like it'd be exhausting, but the long day of travel has my thighs quaking as he helps me off the seat.

"What can I do to help?" I ask.

He gestures to the dust-mobile. "Retrieve our rations for the night from the side compartment. I will set up the vacuuroom."

I nod wearily, wishing I had his endurance, but I've never been able to do much for very long, not even when I had medications back home. Packed away in neat little sections are a variety of what looks like freeze-dried food in metal boxes. I select two of them, not caring what they contain, just knowing I'm starving.

"Is the food out here really not edible?" I ask as I join him by the already erected tent of sorts. Galen mentioned it, but only briefly. The land may be desert and mountains, but there are trees interspersed throughout the dunes and throughout the journey I caught the shadow of animals moving from time to time.

"Once it has been tested and cleared, we can eat a lot of the meat," he explains. "We try to grow our own plants in a safer environment, well away from the radiation."

Calix helps me to the vacuuroom with one hand bracing my elbow. The structure stands maybe five by seven feet and I come to a startled halt at its entrance, my eyes bulging.

Turning to him, I say, "How in the world did that fit on the dust-mobile?"

"Dust-mobile?" he repeats. When I gesture to the vehicle, he nods in understanding. "It is collapsible technology Oz developed with Jareth. It is really quite remarkable."

"I'll say."

Calix uses his armband at the door much like they did at the facility. With a beep and a whirring sound, the door springs open into a small decontamination room where we remove our outer suits and helmets, leaving us in the skintight minnasuits underneath.

He presses a command on a keypad in the wall and the second door opens. Oz and Jareth must be friggin' geniuses because if I didn't know any better, it would feel as though we were in one of the rooms at the facility.

"This is incredible," I whisper.

"I hope it eases your worries about traveling."

I give Calix a wry smile. "I guess I wasn't too good at hiding it."

Calix lifts a hand to caress my cheek. "I do not want you to hide anything from me, lilapetal."

Hopefully he can't see my nervous gulp. I smile hesitantly. "So, what's for dinner?" I ask instead of bringing up the one thing I know will take away the loving look he sends me.

My secret.

Something I'm terrified for him to find out.

[ 8 ]

CALIX

HER MOOD HAS CHANGED and I can sense it. I can see it. I can practically taste it. But then she shifts her blue eyes away from mine, hiding her thoughts from me. All it does is make me want to pull them straight from her, destroy the bad ones and coddle the good ones.

"Ahh, good choice," I praise as I begin prepping the meal packets. I am distracted from my task as I watch her settle on a cushion, tucking her thin legs beneath her. Her skin is pale and I am not pleased with the dark smudges under her eyes. She seems weakened from our travels. Quickly, I prepare our food and hand her the one that is most palatable.

"Thank you," she rasps, her smile thin and forced.

My brows furrow as I regard her. I barely register

inhaling my food as my attention is solely focused on her as she nibbles at her meal. "When you finish eating, I would like to check your vitals."

Her panicked eyes fly to mine. "I'm fine. We should rest."

"Your vitals will determine how long we rest, Emery."

She nods in resignation and tears well in her eyes. I search her face, but she turns her nog to look out the window to avoid my gaze. Her fingertip runs along the glass and she lets out a heavy sigh. "I feel like I am suffocating."

Often, these little aliens say things that have other meanings. And since she's not clutching at her throat for air, I assume she means she feels trapped. "This is not the facility and we're no longer with our faction," I tell her gently. "We are on Mortuus, free to travel about as we see fit."

She swipes the heel of her hand over her cheek-bone, erasing the evidence of her tears. "Not figuratively, Calix. Literally. I didn't want to say anything..." she trails off and a sob catches in her throat. "I feel like I'm dying too quickly and nothing is slowing it down. If anything, I feel like I'm on borrowed time."

I prowl over to her and move the tray of food from

her so I can cradle her face with my hands. "I will not let you die." The growl that rumbles from me is fierce and terrifying, but it is so convincing, even I nearly believe it.

"Promise?" she chokes out, her hands gripping my wrists as though I might vanish from her sight.

"On my own life," I vow.

The sadness bleeds from her as her expression changes from one of worry to desire. Her nostrils flare, a slight pink burns across her cheeks, and her supple lips part. When she licks them, I let out a groan, remembering how sweet she tastes. Desperate for another sample of my lilapetal, I lean forward and press my mouth to hers. She moans and it stirs my cock to life.

"Calix," she breathes as she climbs into my lap. Her legs straddle me and her kisses intensify. I love the way she runs her fingertips through my messy hair. "I need you."

"What do you need me to do?" I ask, my voice hoarse.

She rolls her hips, grinding her center against my cock through our suits. Pleasure surges through me and my hands grip her waist in warning.

"I need you to make love to me..." she trails off, her

breath hot against mine. "I don't want to die without being with you. It's irrational to you, I'm sure, but I'm yours if you'll have me."

I kiss her deeply until she seems to melt within my arms. So soft and trusting. I could spend eternity adoring her. "You want to mate with me?" I clarify, making sure I understand her intentions both spoken and unspoken.

"Yes," she insists, nipping at my bottom lip in a playful way.

I grin and trail kisses along her jaw to her cute little ear. "Our people mate for the purpose of reproducing."

She lets out a soft chuckle. "And my people mate sometimes just for pleasure."

"Pleasure?" My words are husky. I know her meaning. So often I have lain in bed, tugging at my cock and given in to the throes of one-fisted passion. I know what she insists on us doing will bring pleasure to me. But I am hoping she will find pleasure too.

"Yes," she says, smiling. "You might have to get me off first to get me ready. Like you did in the lab."

My cock twitches at the reminder of how I brought her to climax with my fingers. "Then this," I murmur, tugging at the zipper on the back of her minnasuit, "needs to go. It hinders in our plans to mate."

Her cheeks redden, but she nods, a wide grin on

her face. I love that color has been brought back to her features. It reminds me that she is alive and mine and here right now.

"Your skin is unlike anything I have had the pleasure of touching before," I utter as my clawed fingertips gently slide down her spine.

She shivers and pushes closer to me, the globes of her breasts smashing against me. It does nothing to help calm the state of my cock. If I am not careful, I will spill my seed just from a few simple touches.

"Let me see you." I lift my gaze to meet hers. She bites on her bottom lip as she allows me to pull down the front of her suit, baring her breasts to me. "You're so beautiful."

"So are you," she whispers.

Unable to stop from touching her, I lean forward and press my lips between her breasts. Her heart steadily beats against my mouth. I will check her vitals later with my machine, but I can easily make sure she is well with a few simple tests.

Heartbeat—steady and rhythmic.

Temperature—warm and normal.

Breathing—rapid and raspy, but not too labored.

I splay my palm on her back and reposition us so she is lying down and I am above her. She is too delicate to bend her over and mate properly with her.

99

According to the manual about mating—the one every mort has worn the pages of obsessing over—detailed out how you take your female from behind. With my lilapetal, though, we will make adjustments to accommodate her needs. She's far too weak to be taken so roughly. Her breath hitches—in a good way—when I begin kissing her breasts. Slowly, with lips only at first, but when I start licking and sucking at her nipples, she lets out a moan and rips at my hair.

"Calix," she whimpers.

The tone of her voice is needy in nature. It spurs me on to continue tasting her. I kiss down her soft stomach and dip my tongue in the hole she has there. She lifts her bottom when I peel the minnasuit farther down. Her sweet scent floods my nostrils the moment her cunt is exposed to me. The blond curls she has there make me want to bury my nose in them to mark my skin with her scent.

She giggles and my gaze snaps to hers.

"Something funny?" I tease with a half grin.

"You're growling," she says, her eyes glimmering with trust.

"My female brings out the beast in me."

She simply smiles at me as I completely rid her of her suit. "Take yours off too, Calix. I want to see my alien."

I do not remind her that she is the alien because she seems proud of her claim on me. I will let her call me whatever the rekk she wants as long as she looks at me with those pretty blue eyes and wears that lovely smile.

The removal of my suit is less gentle. A little feral in fact. Normally, I am careful not to puncture my suit or tear the seams. This solar, I practically rip it from me. When my heavy cock bounces out, her brows lift as she blatantly studies it.

"I hope it is to your satisfaction," I say with a hint of smugness. I have watched her long enough to learn the meaning of her expressions. This one she is wearing now is the same one she has when she is hungry. The way she licks her lips sends a thrill shooting through me. I catch another whiff of her sweet scent and let out a groan.

"Make love to me," she commands, her gaze still on my cock.

"I would like to taste your cunt first. The scent makes my mouth water," I admit. "Please."

She giggles. "Well, since you asked so nicely." Her thighs pull apart and she reveals herself to me. Like the bud of a lilapetal, her petals open for me, revealing a pink center.

I grip her thighs and pull her farther apart before

running my nose along her wet slit. The nub she likes touched seems to throb with need. I lick it, sending her back arching off the cushion.

"Yesss," she moans. "Do that again."

Eager to please my mate, I swirl my tongue in the same spot over and over again. The sweet nectar is delicious and I could grow addicted to it. Similar to how our commander is addicted to the sun. I am addicted to my mate's cunt. I become ravenous and am no longer satisfied with simply licking her nub. My tongue laps at her opening, where her sweet juices leak from her. The more I suck and taste her, the more she thrashes in a delightful way.

"More, oh God, Calix!"

Her pleas and moans spur me on. At one point, I get a little into pleasing her that I am not careful with my double fangs. When I taste her metallic blood, I freeze.

"Emery," I hiss against her thigh where her blood beads.

"It's okay," she whimpers. "It feels good."

When I suck at the blood on her thigh, just near her cunt, she moans so loudly I am afraid she will lure predators to us. What I am doing is incredibly unsanitary, yet I cannot stop sucking at the tiny hole I have created. Her taste is maddening. I somehow manage to unlatch my mouth from her small wound and bring my attention back to her nub. I suck on it like I want to suck on her wound. She especially likes it when I run my forked tongue on either side of her nub based on the way she screams. Soon, she is shuddering as though she is suffering from a bad case of The Rades. Her sweetness leaks from her body and I eagerly lap it up.

"Oh my God," she rasps. "That was the most amazing thing ever."

I pull away from her and grin. My face is wet from her juices—juices that I am eager to have dripping from my cock.

"Did Aria tell you what it feels like when we release our seed?"

Her eyes widen. "No. Does it hurt?"

"Not at all. In fact, you become..." I trail off. "The toxica that is present in our seed has paralytic effects. Are you...do you still want..."

"Will you protect me?"

"Rekking always," I growl.

She smiles and her lashes bat against her cheeks. "Then I trust you. I want it to feel good for you."

"Just being with you is good enough."

Her fingers dig into my biceps as she pulls me to her. "I don't want it to be good enough. I want it to be the best thing you've ever felt in your life."

My body settles on hers. I love the way she feels so tiny beneath my larger, stronger frame—as though I am the only one who can ever protect her. She is mine to adore and look after. Mine. I rub my cock through her slickness and against her nub, wetting it.

"You are such a giving mate," I praise, my mouth eager to lock with hers once more. I brush my lips over hers as the head of my cock pushes against her opening.

"Maybe I'm a greedy mate," she teases. Her heels push into my buttocks as she urges me inside her.

I let out a groan of pleasure as I thrust my hips and drive all the way into her tight, tiny body. She cries out, her nails digging into my flesh, but she does not push me away. Her arms lock around my neck and her lips press to mine.

"Make love to me, Calix."

Her words stoke a fire inside me. I give in to my animalistic instincts to mate and buck wildly against her. She roams her hands all over me, but I want them in mine. I grip them and pin them to the cushion on either side of her nog. Slightly, I lift up so I can watch her as I mate with her. Our bodies are making slurping sounds, but her moans are a song for my heart.

"You are so wet and tight inside," I grunt. "It feels

so good. I think I may not be able to refrain from spilling my seed."

"Why would you ever want to refrain?" she whispers.

I groan as my release rushes through me. My seed fills my lilapetal up to the brim. A strong sense of male pride ripples from me as I conclude my seed will unite with hers, making us a little mortling of our own. I grunt until I have emptied every last drop and then I fall against her, careful not to crush her.

"Shhh," I breathe as I kiss her pink nose. "Let me take care of you now."

I had expected panic like Breccan had mentioned, but not Emery. Her blue eyes shine with trust and adoration. She is unable to move and I am locked inside her. I could see how that might be frightening.

But not my dear, brave mate.

Her blue eyes burn with fire and determination.

She is a fighter.

And whatever is ailing her, we will fight together. Together, we will heal her.

"My heart only beats for you," I murmur against her soft lips. "It never beat until you. You give me life, my fragile lilapetal."

A tear leaks down her temple.

"Do not worry," I coo, understanding the worried

thoughts going on in her nog without her having to voice them. I am that in tune with her. "As long as your heart beats, so will mine. And if yours ceases to beat, mine will too. Whatever happens, we will do it together. In this life or the one after."

[ 9 ]
EMERY

WHAT CAN ONLY BE THUNDER, cracks and then *booms* and I shoot awake. The heavy weight of Calix's arm falls with a thump in between us. The vacuuroom that had seemed so sturdy yesterday sways precariously in the howling wind. For a moment, my thoughts can't quite catch up, my brain still languid with the aftereffects of the paralytic—toxica he'd called it—and the stupor of near-drugged sleep. Then, the lightning strikes again, closer, louder, and I stumble to my feet to the doors.

I peer through the small port-like window and the view on the other side causes my heart to drop to my feet. The storm that had seemed so far away the day before is right over us. It boils like an angry red-orange tornado, except it's as wide as the horizon and threaded with violent bolts of lighting and I don't even know what else.

We have to leave.

Now.

My knees cry out in protest as I throw myself to Calix's side. "Calix, wake up. We have to go."

He murmurs in his sleep and reaches an arm up to wrap around my waist. Then my words seem to sink in and his eyes snap open, dark and as stormy as the sky outside. His gaze flashes to the window and he's on his feet so fast I come unbalanced and fall on my hands.

Cursing under his breath, or at least, I guess it's cursing for morts, he tosses clothes in my direction. "You must dress. We'll have to travel alongside the storm until we find a break or shelter."

"We can't stay here?" I ask, even as the structure whines violently. I dress in the minnasuit and then the zu-gear as quickly as possible. It's not until I join him at the entrance that I realize I'm not out of breath. On any other day, the adrenaline, the panic and rushing around would have reduced me to a wheezing mess.

I don't have time to give it any thought because an explosion of sound crashes right outside the door and I let out a screech of terror. "Calix?"

He's dressed in his own gear and gestures for me to precede him through the door. Wind—harsh and unrelenting—assaults us hard, nearly knocking me off my own feet. Luckily, Calix is strong and is able to guide me to the vehicle. "Get on and wait for me."

I shake my head, my gaze full of the growing storm. "No, let me help you."

Calix tips my chin up with a clawed finger. "No, lilapetal. I want you where I can keep you safe. Stay here. I'll be back."

He waits until I've buckled myself in the dust-mobile, which I do without further protest because arguing will only take longer, then he jogs back to the structure. I take my eyes off him only to glance at the rumble of clouds. It had been so easy to forget the dangers that lurked outside of our little sanctuary while his hands were on me, so easy to lose myself in the mastery of his touch. Was this, like my illness, a punishment?

Calix returns a few tense minutes later, revs up the dust-mobile, and we shoot into the shadowy tendrils of clouds. I'm in charge of holding onto his zenotablet that guides us on where to go.

I don't speak for a while, letting him navigate the treacherous terrain without distraction with my heart pounding in my throat.

"Do not worry, sweet-one. Everything is going to be fine."

Whatever response I was going to have is cut off by the thunderous roar of noise that fills the protective bubble of the dust-mobile. I slap my hands over my head and fold myself in two, trying to take up the least amount of space possible. My first thought is entirely selfish. *No, I'm not ready to leave yet.* Then, my worry shifts to Calix. Is he hurt? Beside me, I hear him grunting and cursing, then another tremendous roar and a loud *clap* that I can feel deep down in my bones.

"Magnastrikes," I hear Calix shout as the dust-mobile begins to jerk wildly. "Stay down."

I want to look up to make sure he's okay. I want to reach out a hand to touch him, but my muscles are locked with indecision.

The dust-mobile runs over something, throwing me into the air, then slamming me back down on the seat with enough force that I bite clear through my lip. Blood and saliva pool in my mouth, drip down my lips and onto the visor, splattering across my field of vision. I brace one hand on the dash in front of me to stabilize as we crash and bump across rocky terrain.

I have one second where I turn my head and see a flash of Calix against the angry red sky, then I'm thrown against the dash and all goes dark.

THE SCENT of burnt plastic and hot metal fills my nose, even with the protective helmet and rebreather, causing me to wheeze and choke as I struggle back to consciousness. The parts of me that had been so sated with pleasure from last night now scream out in protest as I try to push myself upright. Blinded by the blood pooled on the inner portion of my visor, I suck in a deep breath and detach it. Then, I carefully set up the external rebreather, designed somewhat like a diver's apparatus, that covers my mouth and nose. My lip is still bleeding, but it's begun to clot. Without the bloodied visor, I peer through the shadowy interior of the dust-mobile, hoping to find Calix uninjured.

Please, let him be okay.

"Calix?" I call out, my voice wobbly and distorted from the external rebreather. "Are you all right?"

Ropes of wire and insulation drape down from the ceiling like ghostly intestines and I claw my way across them to get to his side. I find him slumped against the shattered window, unconscious.

"Calix?" I reach out a tentative hand and gently shake his shoulder. "Wake up. We have to keep moving."

The storm is right on us. We have to get our ride repaired and get back on the road as soon as possible before it's too late. Climbing across the center console,

I perch awkwardly as I survey his injuries and the overall damage.

Aside from what looks like a head injury of sorts, Calix doesn't seem to be bleeding from anywhere else, but I'm no doctor and head injuries can be serious. Impotent tears leak from my eyes as I take off his own visor and clamp the external rebreather to his mouth so I can better asses his wounds, even though I know there's next to nothing I can do about them.

I mop up the blackish-red-colored blood on his face as best as I can with a spare bit of cloth I find. The large gash near his temple is leaking blood more freely than makes me comfortable, so I tie a makeshift bandage around it. That's the best I can do for now, until I make sure we're both safe from the storm. I don't know how the hell I'm going to do that, but I'll have to think of something.

It takes several tries, but I manage to get the door on my side open, though it's damaged and will only open halfway. I squeeze out in my suit and do a quick study of our surroundings.

At first, I think it's the dark cast from the clouds that's making everything seem so dark. Before, they'd been so thick and so opaque they'd blotted out any light from the sun other than the eerie red glow. Then

I realize it isn't clouds blocking out all the light, it's rock. Thick, towering rock.

Calix had driven us straight into a cave.

I want to laugh. In fact, it bubbles up in my chest, but I clear my throat and force myself to focus. Just because we're in this cave, doesn't mean we're safe yet. We need shelter, food. Calix needs that cut doctored before it gets any worse.

I give myself short, easy-to-follow instructions. *Get out the vacuroom, Emery. Find a suitable location to set it up, Emery.* Then I take fifteen long, agonizing minutes to figure out how to get the damn thing to open and waves of relief course over me when all it takes is the simple push of a button. Just like Jareth explained. It springs open and unfolds itself. Moments later, the structure is complete.

*You have to get him inside where it's safe, Emery.*

I go back to the dust-mobile and rally my strength and focus on getting Calix to the shelter. He's got a good hundred pounds on me, and all the exertion and excitement already has me feeling weak and light-headed.

Another bolt of that charged, murderous red lightning flashes, spurring me into action. Rushing back to the vacuuroom, I grab what I need before going back to Calix. Using one of the blankets from our bedding, I arrange it at the foot of the driver's side and carefully open his door without letting him fall out. His dead weight crashes into me, knocking out what little breath I have, but I don't have time to focus on me. He is my priority.

I had nothing before I met Calix and meeting him has given me everything. Losing him would be worse than being alone. Having that slice of happiness and having it be ripped away is unthinkable. I've finally met someone I connect with.

I could get used to it being just the two of us.

No matter what planet we're on.

I never thought it'd be with an alien, but when I look at him, I don't see the forked tongue and pale skin. I see the man who looks at me like I'm the key to his happiness.

And I'll be damned if I lose that now.

It takes longer than I like and Calix groans in pained protest as I maneuver his body out of the dust-mobile and onto the thick blanket. His head wound is bleeding profusely, but he's still breathing based on the rhythmic and reassuring sound echoing in our comms.

"Almost done, baby. We just have to get you inside and we'll be okay," I tell him.

White spots dance along my vision, but I grit my teeth and get back to my feet. Gripping the blanket tight in both hands, I begin to heave it backward toward the vacuuroom. I have to pause several times on the edge of losing consciousness, but I fight to keep myself upright and drag him in fits and starts into the shelter and away from the storm. The decontamination process is an easy press of a button that sprays off the harmful toxins on our suits before giving us a healthy burst of air to dry us. It takes some wrangling, but I manage to remove both of our zu-gear, masks, and boots. Now that I can't hear his breathing in the mask, I am worried. I feel a fluttery pulse under my fingers when I press my hand to his throat. He's still alive.

"We made it. We're safe."

I know he can't hear me, but I keep talking as I work him the rest of the way in the vacuuroom and lock up the doors behind us. I'm not sure how bad it's going to get or if we're even safe, but if the force of my will could sway the elements, we will be.

*Food now, Emery.*

I leave him propped against a wall inside our shelter just inside the decontamination area before readying the space for us. I take two of the meals he'd shown me before and manage, I hope, to properly heat them up. Once it and our beds are ready, I go back to Calix.

Bracing myself along the wall of the room, I shuffle

to a bank of shelving where I find more clothes, supplies, and *yes* bandages. Everything is marked in their language, but I take a tube of cream and hope it's an antibacterial salve.

Using a bottle of water and a swath of cloth, I tenderly clean the jagged edges of his wound. It's deeper and bigger than I'd anticipated—the blood had obscured most of it. About four inches long and so deep I swear I see the white of his skull underneath, the wound steals what's left of my breath. Frantic thoughts of brain damage and blood loss assault me, but I keep repeating the directions.

*Clean the wound, Emery.*

*Put on the salve, Emery.*

*Bandage the wound, Emery.*

When I'm done, I sit back on my heels, quivering. I watch him for a few long moments, like my doctoring will have some magical effect and he'll wake if I hope hard enough.

But he doesn't.

My stomach clenches and I force myself to eat the freeze-dried meat and vegetables I prepared, but I don't taste it. I know I'll need to keep my strength up, so I make sure to finish all of it, even licking the tasteless gravy from my fingers. I purify a bottle of water and drink all of that, too.

When there is nothing left to do, I settle down next to Calix and rest my head on his shoulder, hoping a short nap will calm my breathing. Hoping when I wake up, Calix will be better.

Hope is like oxygen. The more I need it, the less my body seems able to absorb.

[ 10 ]

CALIX

THE THROBBING in my nog pulls me from a deep slumber, much to my annoyance. I blink several times to clear away my daze. My memory is fuzzy. Emery starred in my dreams, beautiful but worried. I remember her bringing broth and water to my lips. Assisting me in using the facilities. Sponge bathing me. Mostly, I remember how she clung to me.

I reach for her and the blanket is cold beside me. Panic rises up inside me as I try to shake away the cloud in my nog

What solar is it?

How many solars have passed?

Why does my nog hurt so bad?

I begin to frown and feel a tugging at my temple.

Tentatively, I reach up and touch the tender area that is protected by a bandage.

"Emery," I croak.

Just beyond the vacuuroom, I can hear the wind raging outdoors. We are no longer in the elements, but we are close. I know we never traveled around Bleex Mountain. We were close to it but still two or three solars' worth of travel around the mountain we still had ahead of us.

Rekk.

I remember the crash.

Everything else comes in flashes.

"Emery," I call out, sitting up on my elbows. The pounding in my skull grows worse, but I ignore it as I seek her out.

When she does not answer, my heart ceases to beat. What if she succumbed to her illness? Or a beast decided to make a meal of her? What if she never survived the crash and my memories were not memories at all, but just my soul longing for hers?

I have to get out of here.

It takes everything in me to get to my feet. A wave of nausea roils through me and I stagger into a wall, hitting my shoulder hard. I let out a groan, shake away the daze, and continue for the door into the decontamination chamber. I have enough sense in me to struggle into my zu-gear, my books, and my protective rebreather under my mask attached properly before exiting.

As soon as I am out the door, I take in the scene around me. We seem to be inside a cave. I come to the realization that Emery did all this alone. While I was injured and unconscious, she saved us. Pride surges through me. My lilapetal is a fighter. I just hope she keeps fighting.

"Emery," I call out again.

I walk past the vacuuroom toward the mouth of the cave. The storm is violent outdoors and I hope she did not decide to go out there. It would be suicide. Turning from the storm, I make my way past the vacuuroom deeper into the cave where it darkens. Something glows beyond, so I follow the light. It leads into a narrow crevasse tall enough for me to walk through and wide enough for two morts to walk side by side. It seems awfully unnatural.

"Emery!" I bellow her name when I see her slumped on the floor of the cave. No mask. Just an external rebreather. Panic threatens to consume me, but I cannot worry about those things now. I need to focus on one problem at a time. Crouching beside her, I take her nog in my gloved hands, tilting her face up. Her eyes are closed and she's too pale. When her lids flutter, relief floods through me. I am not too late.

I am weak and my nog has turned to a maddening thunder, but all I care about is her wellbeing. I am not strong enough to carry her, but I am able to get her to her feet and rouse her enough so she can stand. Together, we hobble back to the vacuuroom. Once inside the safety of the makeshift facility, I begin stripping away our zu-gear after the rigorous decontamination process.

Her eyes close and she nearly collapses. I gather her in my arms, dragging her through the door into the main room and over to our bed. Once I have her settled and comfortable, I set to gathering my supplies. A quick check of her vitals tells me she's not doing well at all.

Rekk!

I am overcome with defeat and slump beside her. Without the equipment I need, she will surely die. The thought is too much to bear. If she passes, my heart will cease to beat. I will die along with her.

Burying my nose in her hair, I try to memorize her scent. My body wraps around her and I try to warm her, as though that will help somehow. It is a lost cause, but it still feels right. All that can be heard is the loud rattling in her chest. After several moments, her voice comes out in the barest of whisper.

"Make love to me."

I lift up, letting out a harsh chuckle. "Emery—"

A shaky finger presses to my lips. "I didn't have a chance to tell you..." She squeezes her eyes shut and coughs hard. The wheeze in her chest is terrifying. "It helps."

"What helps?" I demand, frowning at her.

"When...when we did it..." Tears fill her pretty blue eyes and then race down her temples. "I felt so much better."

"Why didn't you tell me?" I ask gently, pressing kisses to her soft flesh.

"I was afraid to hope," she whispers. "Now, hope is all we have left."

Our eyes lock for a long moment as indecision wars inside me.

"Calix," she murmurs. "Just do it." She goes into a coughing fit that makes my heart nearly cease. "J-Just get your c-cock wet. Do it quickly. I don't have the energy for anything else. Please."

Her pleading does me in. I make haste on removing her minnasuit. Mine gets stripped away in the next instant. When I hold up my palm and frown at it, Emery takes my wrist and draws it to her mouth.

Gently, she pushes out her sweet, fat tongue and licks my palm. My mind nearly detonates with a million simultaneous thoughts about how unsanitary this is. But before I can stop her actions, she is guiding my hand back to my cock. I am not hard until she wraps my hand around my length. Taking over, I stroke myself until I am fully erect while also smearing her saliva all over. I give her a questioning look and she gives me a small nod.

"I am yours," I vow as I gently push into her body. "I will always do your bidding. No matter how unusual your request." Like asking me to mate with her on her deathbed.

She smiles. "I'm yours too."

Gathering my fragile lilapetal into my arms, I pull her up and against my chest as I sit back on my haunches. She rests her nog on my shoulder and her hot breath tickles my neck. I grab her fleshy bottom and urge her body up and down my shaft. Another coughing fit takes hold of her, causing her cunt to clench with each cough. I press my lips to her nog and let out a groan. My release comes quick and easy, knowing this is not about pleasure, but about healing. The sooner I spill my seed, the sooner we can see if it helps any.

We're quiet as the toxica effects spread through

her. She slumps against me. Softly, I stroke her bare back and kiss her nog. I guide us back down onto the bed, but remain inside her. Her blue eyes are wide as she studies my face up close. While she stares, I push her hair from her face and lap away the lingering tears on her cheeks. We remain like this for some time until she begins to feel again. Her body twitches and squirms until she is now stroking my hair.

And smiling.

Big and beautiful.

Perfect.

"Calix," she says, her smile widening. Strong. Her voice is stronger. "We need to get you to a lab."

"How long does it work for?" I ask, my mind already working out tests I want to run on each of us. Blood. Semen. Saliva. I want to run it all against each other under a micro-viewer so I can see what healing properties there may be.

"Well, last time, the storm wiped me out. And then the accident. Maybe a few hours I felt really good," she tells me. Her brow lifts. "You look pretty wiped out, though."

"I am fine," I assure her.

"But we can use the microbot thingies to help heal you." Her brows are furled with concern that makes my heart surge with pride.

"Nonsense. I will save those for your much-needed surgery."

She lets out a sigh as she concedes. "Okay, but we at least need to get some real food into you."

"This, we can do." I cannot help but grin at her. "And then I'll mate with you in a few hours. To keep your strength up."

"To keep my strength up," she mirrors.

Hope, like a little mortling inside a womb, implants and begins to grow in our hearts.

---

"Are you sure about this?" she asks as she stares into the crevasse.

I nod as I look down at my zenotablet. The geo-positioning sonar program shows that Sector 1779 is directly on the other side of the mountain. Hope tells me that crevasse is not a coincidence. It was too perfectly carved. We cannot go out into the geostorm and around the mountain, but what if we attempted to go through it instead?

"I am hopeful," I tell her, meeting her with a smile.

"Hope's good enough for me."

I memorize her smile before we disappear into the depths of the cave where it will be cold. After another mating after dinner, she is pink-cheeked and breathing easily. I absolutely must get to a lab and run these tests. Until then, we will make do.

Even if that means I have to take her against a cave wall every few steps and then carry her afterward while the toxica is healing her broken body.

My cock strains against my minnasuit and I chuckle. "Come now, lilapetal. Time is of the essence."

I shoulder our pack and take her hand in mine. She shines the light into the tunnel and we make our way into the darkness while I read the geo-positioning sonar.

Hope leads the way.

---

"What are these?" Her fingers reach past me to the cave wall I am leaned against as she runs her dull, useless claws against the rock.

We have stopped dozens of times over the past two solars within the cave just to do this. Mate. Medicinal mating is what we have affectionately taken to calling it. Each time, she waits patiently while I test the R-levels that are always non-existent within the cave. The air inside this cavern has proven to be safe. Now that we are no longer in such a rush, I also take the time to bring her pleasure beforehand. Now that the toxica is finally leaving her system, she is regaining movement in her limbs after our latest mating. And like the curious being I am learning her to be, she is intrigued by her surroundings.

I turn my nog to look at the sparkling gem lodged in the rock that sparkles from the glow of the light we set up nearby. "Ahhh, that is a dizmonyx. Rare, but quite durable. Oz can turn these gems into sharp tools that can cut through anything. They are tough gems, but incredibly beautiful." I look back at her face and kiss her pert nose. "Kind of like you."

Her grin is sweet and happy. I want to make her do that more often.

"Can I have one?"

A chuckle resounds from me. "You can have whatever you want, my mate."

"Your mate, huh?" she teases, returning her fingers to my hair.

"Always," I say with a possessive growl.

Her forehead rests against mine and she lets out a pleased sigh. "Where I come from, they call it marriage."

I am reminded of the ceremony that bound Aria and Breccan. It warms my heart. "Will you marry me like Aria married the commander?"

Her lips quirk up. "Most men would propose from their knees."

"I am not like most men," I tease.

The smile on her face falls and I panic for a moment thinking I chased it away. Her lip wobbles. "No, you're better, Calix. You're better than any man or any alien in the galaxy. You're the best."

I give her a quick peck to her lips and grip her hips to pull her off me. Once I've cleaned her and we redress, I hunt down my pick and small mallet. Her laughter echoes through the cave and I decide it is the best sound I have ever heard.

"Which one?"

She squats and points to one that juts out of the rock. I kneel beside her to take a look. It is mostly sticking out, so it only takes a few hard cracks of the mallet to loosen it. Once I have it in my grasp, I hand it to her.

"Yes," she says, her eyes lighting up. "The answer is yes. I'll marry you."

Before I can respond, we hear a growl.

I am on my feet with her pushed behind me in the next second. Something lurks in the darkness. Sabre-vipes don't venture this deep into the mountains. Something else creeps.

"Whoooo arrrre youuuu?" it hisses just beyond the edge of the light, the voice echoing all around.

"It talks," Emery whimpers.

"Light," I mutter under my breath.

She shuffles behind me and then her small pocket light gets shined toward the source.

"What the—" I start, confused by what I am seeing.

A mort, tall as me but rail thin squints against the light. His black and silver mane is braided and hangs down in front of his chest. White whiskers stick out in every direction along his jaw and cheeks.

"Name," I bark out, my pick still pointing out in front of me in case I need to use it against him to protect Emery.

"Loxxxx."

I cock my nog to the side and pull down my spectacles from the top of my nog, affixing them on the end of my nose to get a better look.

"Phalix?" he croaks out. "Is that you?"

His words are a punch to my chest. "That was my father. I'm Calix."

He barks out a laugh. "Rekk, you got big, son."

"And I thought you were dead, old mort."

[ 11 ]
EMERY

I SHOULD BE grateful we've found someone else, but my smile is wobbly as the two morts lurch forward for a manly embrace. I've been enjoying the alone time with Calix, even if it's been wrought with peril. I'm a bit sad to see it end, considering the risks associated with the upcoming surgery.

One more night, long enough for us to get to the sector and figure out a plan—then I'll tell him. The impulse for honesty after all we've shared is inherently selfish, I recognize that, but I don't want to die and have him find out some other way. The thought of him looking at me with anything other than affection chills me to the bone and I begin to shiver, even though I'm sweating.

"This planet hasn't killed me yet," Lox replies.

"I see your translator is working," Calix tells him and then pauses. "When Sayer delivered the technology and instructions many revolutions ago, we were not sure if anyone would find it or have use for it."

Lox grins toothily. "I found it."

"Who inserted it?" Calix asks, unease in his tone.

His friend, with a wild glint in his eyes, taps the side of his head. "I did it my rekking self."

Calix is quiet for a moment and then chuckles. "I cannot believe you have been here all this time. It is rekking good to see you." I've never seen Calix smile so big before. It must make him remember his dad, considering the two of them worked in Sector 1779 before he died.

"Good to see you as well, my friend. It's been many solars since I've had such a good one. Come, come with me. Sector 1779 is a short walk from these caves. Tell me about your journey along the way."

Lox beckons us forward and Calix follows him without question. I'm much more hesitant, but Calix seems so happy that I ignore my concerns and shoulder my pack more securely.

"My mate and I were stranded by the storm a few solars ago and I did not think we would make it. My mate managed to save us both and we have been traveling through the caves ever since."

"You're lucky, the mountains are often engulfed in these storms. It's why I've been stuck at Sector 1779. I can only travel within the caves or in the facility."

"And you have been here since my father left?"

"I have. It's been a long time." Lox smiles, showing his teeth, blackened from lack of care and his eyes yellowed from spending too much time underground. Both his grin and expression seem a little wild to me, but I attribute that to his being locked away by himself for so long. Anyone could go a little crazy being alone. I, for one, should be able to sympathize.

Plus, it is getting harder and harder to breathe. Even the last time we'd made love didn't help ease the tension in my lungs. It was like trying to suck in oxygen through a straw. No amount of medicinal sex or wishing is doing the trick anymore.

I need to get to Sector 1779 as quickly as possible. Even if it means going with this stranger. Even if it means I'll soon have to face all the things I've been hiding from.

The two of them chatter animatedly as Lox leads us through the catacombs. I don't miss how he keeps glancing back at me. "Is something wrong?" I ask. The morts—aside from when Breccan tried to keep me from Calix—have never really bothered me. In fact, I almost prefer them to humans, but this one makes my skin crawl.

He gives me a lopsided smile. I try not to wince at his crooked, toothless grin. To Calix, he says, "Such a strange creature. Wherever did you find it?"

A rumble fills Calix's chest. "She is not a creature. This is Emery, my mate. She is an alien who has joined our faction at the facility along with several others. It has become necessary to mate with them in order to grow our numbers."

"There are more survivors?" Lox asks with interest, his curiosity about me seemingly forgotten for the moment.

"There are, Lox. Several morts and mates. Once we conclude our business here and repair our transport, we can take you back with us to the facility. The others will be pleased to see you."

"And I, them," he replies. His eyes glow from the light Calix carries.

"How has the surgical bot fared? Is it still operational?" Calix asks.

"It's been many, many revolutions since it's been used, but I've done my best to keep it maintained. I've had to salvage parts to try and repair the comms systems with no success."

Calix nods and glances back at me. He reaches

back a hand to squeeze my own, his eyes growing concerned as he notes my breathing. With a lift of a brow, he expresses his worry, but I shake my head to let him know I don't need to stop.

"What is your interest in the surgical bot?"

"My mate suffers from a breathing condition. I remember Father treating Belin here and how miraculously he healed. We have no other options and"—he glances back at me and lowers his voice—"my mate is deteriorating here. If she does not have this operation, I fear her breaths are numbered."

They devolve into a highly technical discussion about the surgical unit's machines, specifically the bot, and capabilities as we begin to climb a series of crude steps cut into the cave rocks within the mountain. As the altitude increases, breathing gets even harder. I can hear it echoing off the rock walls around me.

To distract myself, I imagine what will happen when Calix is successful at curing me. We'll return to the facility and the other morts. Breccan and Aria will assign us a domicile of our own to begin our lives together. I fidget with the dizmonyx in my pocket. We'll have a little ceremony with the others to cement our commitment. Then, I'll become the best mate, because he deserves it.

From the beginning he's been a dream. More than I deserve.

But if he gives me a chance to have that future with him, I'll do whatever it takes to show him how much I appreciate him and all he's done for me.

I'll spend the rest of my life showing him.

He may be the key to saving my life, but I crave more than that from him.

So much more.

Love, a partner, a mate for life.

The jagged edges of the dizmonyx cut into the palm of my hand. The hope in my chest aches almost as much as my lungs as we reach the top of the incline.

Calix takes my elbow. "Are you well?" he asks.

"I'm fine," I utter, but there's no denying the breathlessness in my voice. He starts to offer to help, but I wave it away. "So, this is Sector 1779?"

Lox opens a rusty looking door set into the rock. "This is the airlock entrance. The filters are still working, so you'll be able to remove your rebreathers."

The door comes open with a metallic clang, causing me to jump. The way the sound reverberates throughout the caves and the shadowed interior with the red light makes it feel like a bad sci-fi flick. I tell myself I'm being silly as we enter behind Lox.

"Let me give you a tour," Lox says. "I'll show you to the surgical unit and the bot first."

Calix follows eagerly behind. "When do you think we can get started?"

"The machines will take a while to be prepped, but I anticipate we can get started as soon as tomorrow morning."

Calix squeezes my hand and I smile weakly. "Thank you, Lox. We will never be able to repay you."

"Transport back is more than enough, my friend."

Lox's thin form leads us through a hallway with flickering orange lights. If the facility's components were decades out of date, Sector 1779 was like stepping through a door into medieval times, if they had access to technology. The walls and doors are made of reinforced steel instead of the indestructible plastic alloy I've grown used to. They clank and groan as we traverse through the hallways, making me think of the old suits of armor knights used to wear.

The surgical unit itself contains a single bed, with a few monitors, dated computers, and machines that look like torture devices. Apprehension churns in my belly and my hands grow clammy.

Noting my concern, Calix turns to me and runs a claw through my hair. "How are you feeling?" he asks as Lox mutters to himself and surveys the machines.

"I'm fine," I answer, but my smile is wobbly. "Maybe a little weak," I admit.

He looks contrite. "I have been so worried about getting here that I did not even consider how strenuous it must be for you. Lox, is there somewhere we can rest? My mate needs to gather her strength before the procedure. While she rests, we can go over what I would like to do, if you do not mind."

"Of course, my friend. Let me show you to our sleeping quarters. It's not much," he warns.

"We will make do," Calix replies.

He isn't wrong. The small, dimly lit room has a small, threadbare cot in the middle. He leaves us there and says he'll meet Calix back in the surgical unit after he retrieves some supplies.

"Just a few solars more and we'll be back home," Calix says, pulling me into his arms.

"Home is wherever you are."

I let him hold me for a moment longer, then pull him down to the small cot. His thick brows crease. "What are you doing?"

"Medicinal mating," I tease, but that's not it. I want to feel him, to feel close to him, one last time in case there aren't any others. He breaks our fall like I knew he would on top of the musty smelling cot, but doesn't kiss back with enthusiasm when I press my lips to his. "What's wrong?"

"You seem as though you are saying goodbye."

I hold him tight against me. "Never."

We'd shed our rebreathers when we entered the Sector, but we shove off our suits with impatient hands. I want to go slow, to savor, to memorize, but the urgency underneath my skin has me pulling him on top of me and stroking him with hands that shake. "Faster," I say as I lick his salty shoulder. "Please."

"Does it hurt?" he asks. His hands make quick work of our suits when mine fail me. "I will make it stop."

"No," I say with a shake of my head. "It doesn't hurt. I just want you. Make me yours."

"You are already mine. We were written in the stars before you set foot on this planet. No matter what happens, Emery. You will always be mine."

I pull him down for a kiss as he enters me with one quick, sure thrust, then I throw my head back. It always feels like the first time with him. The first quick bite of fear that he won't fit, then acceptance as I adjust to fit him. Joy explodes inside of me, like pleasure amplified a thousand-fold. It explodes behind my eyes like a supernova.

The orgasm rolls over me without any prompting

and I gasp its invasion into Calix's neck as the paralysis from the toxica soon follows with his own. He soothes me as he lays me down onto the cot, his hands passing over me in reverence. If I could speak, I would have told him I loved him, but I'm glad I can't. I want to tell him for the first time with a clear conscience.

Tomorrow.

Tomorrow, I will tell him.

He kisses my eyelids when I'm relaxed enough to slip into the floaty place between dreams and reality.

Hope.

It's a powerful drug.

Hope has gotten me through terrible, awful circumstances before. I breathe it in, allowing it to fill my faulty lungs with its life-giving sustenance and let it course through my bloodstream.

Hope will get me through telling Calix the truth.

It will bring me through to the other side of the surgery.

Hope will bring us back to the facility.

If I have anything to do with it, hope will bring us back together again after what I have to say.

I have to believe it.

I cling to hope as I slip into sleep.

[ 12 ]

CALIX

"You're up early," Lox says as he plucks some plump fruit from a bush that is growing from a planter in what appears to be an old nutrition bay.

"We have a busy solar ahead of us." My gaze falls to the fruit. I'm unfamiliar with this one. Seems to be a hybrid of some sort. "What do you have there?"

He flashes me a wide grin, his black irises darting back and forth in a manic way. It reminds me back when Draven had The Rades. I take a quick assessment of my father's old friend to make sure he is not presenting any symptoms.

"This," he says as he tosses the yellow fruit into the air, "is a lembulla." He brings it to his nostrils and inhales. "I crossbred a lemonia tree with grenus root. Between the sweet juice from the lemonia and the nutrients from the grenus, I've been able to mostly survive on these." He tosses it at me and I catch it, my claws puncturing the soft flesh of the fruit.

"I see," I say with a polite smile. "Very clever." When he turns to pick more fruit, I pocket mine and shift my eyes down the corridor where I left Emery sleeping.

Grenus root is something that was eradicated many revolutions ago when it was discovered to have adverse effects on morts. It is known to cause extreme delusions. There are not any nutritious qualities at all. I have read Galen's notes on any and all plant life, both available and unavailable. I remember being fascinated by his notes in that section regarding the grenus root.

Currently, I am not intrigued.

I am worried.

If Lox has been living off this fruit, that means he is unwell. Unpredictable even. I will have to watch him carefully. I would feel better if I had his assistance with her surgery. Without his help, the surgery won't be an impossibility, but will be more difficult. And I don't want that.

"Will you show me where Father performed Belin's procedure?" I ask, keeping my voice normal and unconcerned. The last thing I want is to provoke him if his mind is fragile.

He takes a bite of the lembulla and slurps loudly. The yellow juices run down his chin. Lox doesn't bother wiping it away and it makes me cringe. I follow him down the deteriorating corridor to a large room as he devours his meal along the way. This room is in better shape than the others, which makes me thankful.

We spend the next couple of hours discussing the machines. I am able to connect their purposes with each piece of technology based on my father's notes. Once familiarized with the room, we set to giving it a fresh scrub down, cleaning it from top to bottom. While we work, he asks questions about the facility and our faction. He's especially curious as to how the females arrived in our possession.

"Theron and Sayer," he says as he washes some tools in a basin. "I don't remember them."

"They are several revolutions younger than myself. Probably nothing but nipple sucking mortlings pissing their undersuits when you met them."

"And they have a ship?" he inquires. "I didn't realize those even existed anymore."

I let out a sigh. Lox may be an odd one, looped up on a hybrid hallucinogenic fruit, but he's still one of us. "Yes, the *Mayvina* is Theron's mate."

Lox snorts. "Does his mate ever leave the facility?"

"It is how we..." I trail off. Stole. Aria, Emery, the others. We stole them. "It is how we acquired the females."

"Ahhh," is all he says. "So this metal mate of his. Does she still fly?"

"A little old, but certainly gets out there some."

Theron flies out when the weather is fair to other reaches of Mortuus when we need supplies. Recently we've been made aware of other beings traveling within our atmosphere. Theron and Sayer sometimes do less than honorable things like rob from these vessels. They are skilled and usually are gone with their loot before the beings passing by even realize what hit them. Many times, Theron has brought up to Breccan about catching a ride on one of these larger ships to a new, more habitable planet. But despite our dwindling numbers and lack of females, that world outside of ours is unknown. Unknown creatures, unknown pathogens, unknown air quality, unknown threats. We cannot risk our race over an impulsive whim.

"Can you hand me that carpal knife, Phalix?" Lox asks, nodding his nog to another table.

"Calix," I correct, tilting my nog to the side to study him.

He blinks several times and a shudder ripples

through him. Then, his unusual grin is back on his face. "Calix. I apologize."

While he finishes up, I pull my zenotablet from my pocket and reach for my glasses that have been perched on top of my nog. I place them on the end of my nose and use my stylus to skim through my notes.

"As soon as we perform the procedure, we'll need to ready the terrainster and head back to the facility," he tells me as he dries his old, bony hands.

"It has been smashed to bits, remember?" I told him this last night after Emery had gone to sleep. I told him everything. It is as though he has forgotten our entire conversation.

He blinks at me and then his eyes narrow as though he doesn't believe me. "Nothing a little hard work can't fix."

"We are going to have to find a way to haul it into one of the bays on this side of the mountain. And we certainly cannot do anything until the geostorm clears."

His features screw up into a scowl. "Are there more terrainsters?"

"Back at the facility, but—"

"Then we make communication. We tell your people to rescue us."

*Our* people. I want to correct him, but refrain.

The geostorm is one of the worst I have ever seen. Even if we could communicate with Breccan and the rest, it would be a suicide mission to send them into the heart of this catastrophic storm.

But explaining this to a mort who has been trapped here for countless revolutions, and is half crazed on a lembulla diet, would be wasted breath.

And right now, every breath counts.

*Her* breaths.

My mate.

So, I give him hope. It is all I can offer.

"We will work to make contact after the procedure. Emery will need rest and we can do this while she heals," I tell him, my tone placating.

The flickering in his eyes discontinues and he flashes me another grin. Easy and calm. I try not to flinch each time I see that mouth that is only half-filled with teeth. "Let's get to it, son."

"Lox?"

He approaches and stands too closely. "Yes?"

I mull over how I want to ask this question. It is one that has plagued me for many revolutions. Why did my father leave? Belin was healed. He brought him back. But then...then, he left me. Again. That time, he never came back. Not long after he left, one of the other elders who later caught The Rades and died was the one to discover his body. Nothing but a half-eaten carcass. I was not privy to the details as of how he died. Whether it was a sabrevipe or the elements or illness, I'll never know.

"Why did my father go back here?" I blurt out. "He never made it. I want to know why."

Lox blinks at me several times before answering. "Once Belin was healthy, he wanted to look through some of the other tools and machinery here. See what he could take back with him to the facility. Of course, being his assistant, I went along with him." He lowers his nog. "He never made it."

It is on the tip of my tongue to ask how. How did my father die? But do I really want to know the details? Do I want Lox—already fragile in mind—to relive something so horrific? After my father's death, and Lox's assumed death, he was left to rot in Sector 1779 all alone. Perhaps later I will discuss this with him. Much later. When my mate is healed and we are in the company of the other morts. And where I can have Avrell assist me in weaning him off his beloved lembulla.

"I'm going to fetch Emery," I tell him, clasping his shoulder in an affectionate way. "And the Haxinth."

Luckily, Haxinth was something that Galen, Avrell, and myself were able to concoct. I kept the vials with our rations. With the Sector being old and what we thought was abandoned, finding Haxinth that hadn't rotted was a risk I didn't want to take. Because of Father's notes, we were able to recreate the "living corpse" medicine. The technology is far more advanced at the facility and our microbots usually take care of most of our ailments, but considering the microbots have been a failure on my alien, I could not risk it.

Lox's brows lift. "You have Haxinth?" The greedy glint in his black eyes sends a shiver of unease skittering down my spine. It takes everything in me not to let my sub-bones crack and pop in warning.

"Only enough for the procedure. But back at the facility, more can be concocted," I assure him. I am not sure what his interest is in it. Unless he has some need for that as well. Much like his lumbella. Much like Breccan's sun addiction. I suppose some morts have something they crave, even if it harms them. "What purpose do you have for it?"

He gives me a sheepish smile. "Sometimes I can't sleep. Haxinth helps me sleep."

Like a corpse.

I shudder at that thought.

"I see." I give him a forced smile. "We will make

sure Avrell gets you what you need when you arrive. In due time, friend."

I leave him alone and hurry down the corridor to the room Emery was resting in. I find her sitting on the cot pale and dazed. The raspy wheezing in her chest sends alarm blaring through every nerve ending in my body.

"Lilapetal," I murmur, striding over to her and taking a knee in front of her. "Look at me."

She lifts her nog and her dulled blue eyes meet mine. "Hi, my mate."

My heart warms at her words. I want nothing more than to take her right now. Right here on this cot. But with Lox looming nearby, I do not want to chance it. Besides, she needs this procedure immediately.

"It is time," I tell her. "But I need to warn you."

She presses a cold finger to my lips. "I know there are risks."

"It is not that," I rumble, darting a quick look over my shoulder. "It is Lox. He is unwell." I tap my nog. "Here."

Her lips purse and she nods. "Should we leave?"

"No," I growl. "This surgery is the difference between life and death for you. I need his assistance to perform it. Just be careful. Be wary."

I pull her to her feet and kiss her nose. Her blue

eyes flicker with unspoken words. She bites on her bottom lip with her blunt, useless teeth, as though she can keep her thoughts hidden away from me. I see them brewing, but I do not have time to coax them from her. Time is of the essence.

"Calix," Emery hisses.

"What is it, my mate?"

Her eyes become watery. "I...I..." A single tear leaks out and streaks down her pink cheek.

"Shhh," I murmur. "Do not fear this operation. I will not let anything happen to you."

She swallows, giving me a pitiful look, but simply nods. Quickly, I rifle through my pack for the Haxinth and pocket the vials. Then, I pull her behind me and down the corridor. Inside the room, I find Lox preparing the table. The lights are bright and as we near the table, I discover it is warm.

"Lox," I say upon entering. "Can you leave us for a moment while Emery dresses in a gown?"

He gives me a mock salute and hobbles out of the room, closing the door behind him. I pull an old gown from a drawer. It has been protected from dust but still smells a little peculiar. Since she is so weak, I help her undress and then we get the gown on her.

Once I have her settled on the bed, I withdraw the vial of Haxinth from my pocket and show her. "This will make you fall into a deep sleep. You will not feel a thing," I assure her. "Do you trust me, lilapetal?"

She nods and her eyes grow teary again. Her fingers wrap around my wrist, gripping me tightly despite her overall weakness. "Calix..." Her nose turns pink and she sniffles. "There's something you should know."

I pull her grip from my wrist and bring her palm to my chest. "I know, my mate. My heart beats for you as yours does mine. It will continue to beat, in unison, for many revolutions to come. This solar, you will remain by my side. Just like every solar from here on out."

"Oh, Calix," she chokes out. "That's a declaration of love if I've ever heard one. I love you too. But..."

I frown at her words. "What is it, Emery?"

"There are things you don't know about me. Things I need you to know. It's unfair to you."

"Go on," I urge. "Whatever it is, I am sure it is fine."

She closes her eyes and squeezes out a couple of tears. "That ship...the one we were taken from..."

"Yes?"

"I remember. I know why I was there. I was a prisoner," she whispers. "I...I wasn't kidnapped. It was legitimate." A sob escapes her. "Calix, I'm a criminal. Aria, the others, we're all criminals."

I search my knowledge bank for the meaning of her words. "Clarify."

"I'm not sure what the other girls were there for, but me...I was there because I'm a thief." She lets out a ragged sigh that has me worrying over her lungs. "I stole valuable items from my employer so I could sell them for money. It was wrong, but my medical bills were piling up. And I needed my medications." She swipes away her tears. "I was to do fifteen years, er fifteen revolutions, on a prison planet. Behind bars. Like in one of your reform cells."

It all clicks into place and anger swells up inside me. The sub-bones in my spine crack as I rise to my full, intimidating height. She shrinks away from me, curling into herself on the bed.

"How dare they," I snarl.

She blinks at me in confusion. "W-What?"

"How dare they imprison you for trying to extend your life? Where was their compassion?" I curl my lip up in disgust. "This planet you aliens came from is despicable. It was written in the stars that you ended up here. Where you are safe from those beasts."

A crazed giggle erupts from her. "Y-You're not disgusted with me?"

Leaning forward, I brush away some hair from her face with my claws. "Never. You are the most beautiful and precious thing in this universe. And you are mine."

We kiss once more and then I regretfully break away from her to call Lox back in. He assists me in attaching many different machines to her to monitor her vitals. I ready a needle with the Haxinth.

"I love you, Calix," Emery whispers. "Always remember that."

I hear the finality in her voice. She is not dying this solar.

"I love you, my mate. Sleep now. I will see you soon."

She nods and I waste no time administering the Haxinth. Her eyes grow heavy and then she is asleep a few moments later.

Lox and I move quickly. He suits up in a protective layer before dragging the table over to where she lies still. Living corpse. I despise that description, but it is fitting. Besides her breathing, she remains unmoving. It reminds me of when she was in the pod sleeping for all those solars before Aria woke her.

"You make the incision when I say," I instruct Lox. "I will ready the surgical bot."

His nog bobs wildly. "Yes, Phalix."

"Calix," I correct.

He ignores me and I let out a frustrated breath of

air. It is a real possibility that I may need to kick him out of the room and do it all by myself. It's what I prepared for since I didn't expect him to be here anyway. At the first sign he cannot perform as needed, I will take that action. I will not sacrifice her health.

I sit at the surgical bot machine control panel. The notes my father made were clear and concise. I am able to easily breeze through the workings of it. The arm of the machine groans as it stretches across the room to where my living corpse lies. Through the monitor, I am awarded a close-up view of Emery.

"Draw down the gown. The incision needs to be vertical and between the breasts," I instruct.

"I remember from last time, Phalix," Lox grumbles, irritation in his tone.

With my face pressed against the forehead cushion, I watch with utmost clarity through the monitor as he pulls down her gown. A growl of possessiveness rumbles through me no matter how much I try to retain it. Now is not the time to worry about her virtue. Lox is only trying to help. He lifts a carpal knife and it glints under the light.

*Rekk, please don't hurt her.*

"Not too deep," I remind him.

Lox laughs. Dark and maniacal. I wince when he presses the blade into her pale flesh. Crimson swells from the incision. I waste no time and use the handle on the machine to direct the robotic hand toward the incision.

Time passes too quickly, but the constant, steady beating of her heart that echoes from the machine keeps me focused. It takes more incisions on Lox's part to grant me access to her lungs, but once I'm given entry to the lungs, I'm able to see what it is that plagues my sweet mate.

Her lungs are pink and swollen, but that's not what has alarm ringing through me. It is the webby nodules clinging to the flesh that has me worried. Once, as we lay in bed one night, Emery explained asthma to me.

This...

This is not what she explained.

This is something I understand. Pathogens. Disease. Foreign masses in the body.

Using the clawed end of the robot hand, I carefully hook one of the gray webs and pull. It flickers opaque as though to hide, and it makes me wonder if this is why they did not show up on the previous scans. The unknown parasite tries to cling to her precious lungs, but with tedious tugs, I'm able to free part of the web, sending a splatter of blood across her gown. Perspiration trickles down my temples as I focus. This is nothing like I have ever seen, which makes me wonder if she picked it up on the vessel she was on in space, or perhaps from her own planet. Slowly, I'm able to pull one of the webbed masses from her lungs and to where Lox can grab it with his tool. He tosses it into a container with a splat, sending more blood splattering on him and the floor. Normally, I would be going insane with the mess, but not now. Now, I am solely focused on getting these things out of her body.

One down, only approximately forty or fifty more to go.

I don't have time to analyze what these things are, only that I want them gone.

"It moves," Lox tells me, a slight tremor to his voice. "Slowly, but it is rekking moving."

"Keep a lid on it," I instruct.

Hours and hours pass.

My head pounds, my hand is cramped, and my own lungs are on fire from holding my breath so much. Eventually, I pull the last one free.

"Microbots," I bark out to Lox. They're programmed to heal abrasions, and there are many from where those parasites had leeched onto her. "Now that those masses are gone, I think they'll work."

He begins work using the microbots while I step away from the robotic machine and stretch my back. I make sure the lid is tightly secured on the container holding the parasites that I will study later, and I move it to a table along the wall. He finishes his work and then I take over the delicate task of closing her up. As I'm stitching her, Lox drops his tool and it clatters to the floor, splattering more of her blood. When our eyes meet, his pupils are tiny. The whites of his eyes have nearly taken over, giving him an eerie look about him.

"You're dead," he hisses, taking a step away from us.

I drop my gaze back down to Emery as I continue my stitching. "You need a break, Lox. Take a walk."

"No," Lox barks. "No!"

Panic shoots through me, but I attempt to stay calm. I cannot have him losing his ever rekking mind right now. "Lox," I say slowly. "Why don't you get into my pack and help yourself to some rations?"

He grabs at his unruly white and black locks and tugs. "I sent you to The Eternals. Why are you still here?"

I snap my nog up to glare at him. "What?"

"When you found out I had been using the Haxinth, you told me I couldn't have it anymore. You said you'd put me in a reform cell. To let me detox," he snarls, fury making the sub-bones in his spine snap as he takes a threatening stance. "I needed it. You wanted to take away what I needed."

My blood runs cold as realization rushes through me. Lox. It was Lox. He killed my father and left him to get picked over by predators. It wasn't the elements or illness or a wild beast. It was him. A friend.

"Lox, I am Calix."

He shakes his nog and then tugs his hair in a crazed way once more. I quickly tie off the last stitch and set to wrapping Emery in a medical cloth. Hopefully the microbots will do their job on her external wound because I am afraid I do not have time to monitor them. As soon as I drag the gown back over her bare breasts, I rise to my feet.

"You killed my father?" I growl.

He snarls at me, his claws bared and his eyes manic. "I bashed his skull in with a rock and fed him to a sabrevipe."

Violent fury explodes through me and I pounce on him, sending several zutametal tools clattering to the floor. Emery's bloody gauze from the procedure litters the space. The rekking mort is strong for his old age and manages to punch me in my side hard enough I lose my breath. His claws swipe the air above my face, but I shove at his chest just in time. My fist cracks against his nog, sending it whipping to the side. Before

I can manage another swing, he rolls off me and is on his feet in the next instant.

And then he runs.

I check on my sweet mate, and the moment I feel sure she will be okay, I snatch up a carpal knife, still wet with Emery's blood, and charge after the monster who killed my father.

He will not rekking get away with this.

Sweet, fresh air.

The lack of stones pressing in on my chest.

It's the relief that brings me swimming up from unconsciousness.

I'm unable to move, but I can breathe, so I don't panic. I know Calix must be near and it doesn't hurt, so I let myself swim in the floaty sensation that must be the medication Calix administered.

Calix.

I'd been so worried about my past, so afraid to tell him about the worst parts of me, and he didn't even care. He'd brushed away my fears without a second thought. It was as though he looked into my soul and saw me, the real me, and accepted me, faults and past and all.

I sigh, taking in a deep, long breath of that sweet, fresh air, and imagine Calix's face. With my past and sickness behind us, we can have the future I imagined. Somehow, we'll figure out a way to get back to the others. We made it through the storm once, we can do it again.

---

THE CELL IS SMALL. *Cold. Lonely. I'm shaking and there isn't any room to pace or lie down. Is this my future? Will I spend the next fifteen years standing in a tiny cell starving to death?*

*As if on cue, my stomach grumbles loudly.*

*It's been days since I've last eaten. I'm going insane here. Kneeling, I run my fingers along the bottom of the door where a tiny draft of air swooshes in. I drink from it as though it's actual water. But I'm left empty and parched.*

*Something glimmers, barely sticking inside beneath the door. Leaning forward, I run my tongue along it.*

*Water.*

*God, I am so thirsty.*

*I slurp up the foul tasting, and awfully thick water, and swallow it down. My stupid lungs choose this moment to fail me, sending me into a coughing fit that* has me nearly throwing up the precious drink of filthy water. I manage to keep it down, barely.

What feels like hours or days later, the door finally opens. My captors haul me to my feet and all but carry me to a warm room. Hundreds of tubes are lined along the walls. I'm escorted to one rather roughly. I'm too weak to fight them.

I am pushed into the surprisingly warm and soft standing tube. As they attach tubes to me—tubes that I hope desperately will nourish me—I find myself relaxing. If I have to spend the next fifteen years being punished, I hope it is here, in this tube.

Moments later, something cool slides into my vein and immediately has sleep overtaking me.

---

I COME TO, pushing away my bad memories, and remember where I truly am. At Sector 1779. With Calix. In small increments, the sensation and movement seeps back into my muscles. I can see why Avrell cautioned about the Haxinth. The lack of control is debilitating, but it reminds me somewhat of the paralyzing toxica I'm subjected to when we mate, so it doesn't make me panic. It only reminds me of Calix, which is soothing, but I'd rather see him, touch him. Reality, I've learned, it so much better than dreams.

But where is he?

It's awfully quiet.

I take in the gradual return of feeling starting with my toes. I flex and relax them until I can wiggle them all. Then, I do the same with both feet until movement is back up to my calves. I continue flexing and relaxing all the muscles in my legs. It occurs to me I should worry about feeling returning to the operation site, but the medication has me so tranquil, I resolve to deal with that as it comes. Finally, I can move my hands and arms, then my mouth. Last, my eyes flutter open.

Everything is blurry at first and it takes a minute for my vision to adjust to the brightness from the lamps shining down on the bed. A finger of disquiet traces down my spine, but I'm not sure why at first. I attribute it to coming down from the drugs and the after effects of the surgery.

With a hand, I probe where I estimate the wound in my chest should be. How long has it been since they put me under? Days? Weeks? Certainly not months. Recovery, I imagine, would take a while, but the Morts, even here at the outdated satellite post, have incredibly sophisticated tools. My fingers find the puckered edges of a freshly healed scar through some gauze. Once I assure myself I'm not in any danger of aggravating the wound, I push myself to a sitting position and look around, eager to find Calix.

But the room is empty.

Save for the medical equipment and the table on which I'm sitting, there's nothing else.

The sense of unease increases. Prior to the surgery, it would have sent me into a fit of epic proportions, ending with me passing out, but now, I only begin to breathe more heavily.

Where is Calix?

Glancing around, I note several things that don't seem to make sense. Wouldn't they have put me in a room to recover and monitor me? They wouldn't have left me on the operating table in the surgical room. My eyes focus and my vision fills with blood. On the table where I lie, on the outfit I'd dressed in before the surgery, even on the floors.

But that doesn't make any sense. How could there still be blood if my wound has already turned into a scar? I scoot to the edge of the seat, careful to not step in blood, and slip as I stand on wobbly legs.

"You're awake," comes a voice that makes me do just that.

I yelp and hold on to a monitor of some sort to keep myself upright. My eyes go to a figure in the doorway, but I know before my eyes focus on him that it's not Calix. "Lox?" I ask, my voice hoarse as a frog croak. "Where's Calix?"

His eyes are brighter and more unfocused than ever. At first, I think maybe the surgery took many hours and he needs some rest. "Phalix isn't here anymore. Come with me, we must get to the terrainster and return to the facility before it's too late."

Confused, I follow him as he turns abruptly and marches away. Not wanting to be left behind, I hobble down the hallways barefoot and in my bloody gown. From what I can recall, he's going back to the staircase that leads into the bowels of the mountains.

"Come," he says over his shoulder. "We must hurry."

"Lox, where's Calix? Lox!"

He's muttering to himself, but not answering. It's as though he only barely recognizes I'm there. Fear spears into my chest. Did he do something to Calix? I'm afraid to stop following him. What if he has? If I run away, will I ever be able to find my way back? My head is still cloudy from the drugs and my body is weak, but I have to be strong.

I strain to listen above the sound of our feet slapping against the steel floors, but I don't hear Calix anywhere. There's only me and the mad rantings of Lox.

"No matter how many times I kill him he keeps coming back. No matter, I'll kill him every solar from now until eternity if that's what it takes."

My stomach drops. Is he talking about Calix? If he is, what he's saying isn't making any sense. He couldn't kill Calix more than once, unless he hadn't done it properly the first time. "Kill who?"

But Lox isn't paying any attention to me other than to reach behind and grab my hand when I slow down. His fingers lock around my wrist like shackles and he nearly pulls my arm from the socket. My feet scrub against the slippery floors without finding purchase.

"Lox, stop! Stop!"

"Get the ship and leave this planet for good. I'll make it through the storm if I have to."

He's much bigger and stronger than me. Even with the ability to breathe normally, I'm no match for him. He tugs me down the corridors until we reach the massive outer doors. There, he shuts us into the airlock and puts on his rebreather. When I fight him, he cold cocks me without a moment's hesitation and everything goes dark for a few seconds.

Lox is keying in the code to open the outer door

when my vision comes back. The mask is secured on my face and he somehow got me wrangled into some over-sized zu-gear that feels scratchy against my skin without a minnasuit underneath. It wasn't the same zu-gear I was wearing before. This one is too long in the arms and legs.

Once the door opens he takes me by the arm again and jerks me down the long descent into the red-dark haze of the tunnels. I can't help but feel like he's leading me into the depths of hell. I survived surgery on an alien planet, but will I survive this?

I've got to, for Calix.

I give up pleading with Lox. If he even hears me, he doesn't care. It's like he's not present, really. He keeps mentioning Phalix, Calix's father. The past and the present must have swirled together in his brain.

Maybe it's the drugs, but as we descend deeper and deeper into the caverns, I don't succumb to panic. I don't have a plan, but I know at the first opportunity I'm going to try to escape. He and Calix must have gotten into an altercation during my surgery. I assume they'd given me something to make me heal so quickly. The microbots Calix had mentioned? If so, those things really are something. Later we'll have time for all the answers. Later, when we're safe.

We make the trek back much more quickly than I had with Calix because I don't need to stop to rest every few hours. Too quickly. I'd hoped Calix would find us before we got there, but I haven't seen or heard a sign. Part of me is afraid Lox killed him, but I shove that fear deep down inside me.

The alcove where we'd smashed the terrainster into the mountain is different than when we left it. Lox must have been busy when we were distracted or while I was unconscious because there are piles of tools and spare parts. Guts of the terrainster spill out from its undercarriage and the cracked windows have been repaired with some sort of epoxy.

He's going to escape and abandon us here.

I can't let that happen.

"Phalix won't desert me again. He thinks he controls me, but we'll see how he likes spending solars upon solars alone," Lox is saying as he shoves me in the terrainster and buckles me in. "You wait here and don't move."

Everything inside me is telling me to run, to leave before I'm locked for an eternity with this lunatic, but I force myself to wait. If I escape now, he'll catch me in a second. I may be healed, but I don't know how much I can push myself so soon after surgery. I have to wait for the perfect moment.

Tears want to escape, but I suck them back. We made it through the storm, through my surgery. We'll make it through this. I will find Calix and we'll get through all of this together, even if it means just the two of us alone in this big mountain.

Lox ambles to the other door and boosts himself into the driver's seat. I can feel the window of escape shrinking with each passing second.

*Please. Please let it not work. Let it still be broken.*

But the terrainster starts and purrs as smooth as I imagine a baby sabrevipe would.

The gleam in Lox's eye brightens, but it's not from the lightning. Mere seconds separate me from never seeing Calix again. I don't imagine I'd make it back to the facility with Lox alive. I'd rather run in the geostorm naked.

The best time to make a move would be when he's focused on driving out of the alcove and back into the storm. The radiation lightning flashes so brightly it's nearly blinding. It would be the perfect distraction. Risky. Terribly risky. Calix will probably kill me later for even thinking of it, but I have to try.

For him.

Lox carefully maneuvers the terrainster and over the sounds of the geostorm, I can hear the terrible sound of metal grinding against metal. There's still something broken, but Lox doesn't seem concerned, not that he's anything to judge by. I can only hope the damn thing won't explode before I manage to escape.

I begin to count the number of flashes and the length in between them. They're sporadic, but generally follow the explosions of radiation gasses. When we reach the exit to the alcove, I carefully, slowly unbuckle while Lox is distracted by the uneven terrain.

The moment Lox pauses at the exit, a loud *BOOM* rattles the terrainster. This is my chance. I throw open the door and launch myself through it as lightning flashes. It does so only a second after I make my move, allowing Lox to grab hold of my leg. I scream as the terrainster comes to a rocking stop.

"Get back here, mutt!" Lox snarls.

My body crashes into the unforgiving metal frame. I try not to think about what the impact will do to my freshly healed wounds. "Like hell!" I shout back.

I scissor my feet, kicking at his grasp on my ankles. He howls in pain as I grind his wrists against the center console. I may not have on boots like him, but I have motivation and adrenaline on my side. Jerking my foot back, I slam it into his wrist again and again until his grip loosens.

I crash to the ground with a bone-jarring thump as Lox puts the terrainster in park. I cower and scuttle back inside the cave, away from Lox and the storm. He pauses halfway out of the cab, but I don't understand why until a vicious roar fills the cave.

"LOX!"

Relief and horror fill me in equal measure. "No!" I shout to Calix, who is barreling across the alcove, his face filled with rage. He doesn't seem to hear me.

"You mad old mort. If you cease your foolish actions now, I will show you mercy. Mercy you did not show my father," he says to Lox, who kicks dirt at Calix's feet.

"I'll do no such thing."

Before either of us can react, Lox throws his door shut, then reaches across and shuts mine. He revs the engine and spits rocks on his exit from the cave.

There's a split second where Calix could chase after him. With his exceptional speed, he could have leapt onto the back of the terrainster and fought Lox for control. It was our only hope at returning to the facility. His only hope of being reunited with his faction, but he stands his ground.

Without hesitating, he turns to me and scoops me into his arms. His face nuzzles into my throat. It takes me a moment to realize the shaking I'm feeling isn't coming from the thunderous booms from the storm, but from Calix himself, who can't seem to stop quivering in relief. He falls to his knees.

"I thought I lost you," he says, his voice barely above a whisper.

"I'm okay. I'm right here."

"He attacked me, then disappeared. I tracked him to the caves and searched, but he knew them too well. I failed you, my lilapetal."

If I'm Calix's lilapetal, then he's my sun. On this strange planet, I only feel safe when bathed in his warmth.

I lift his chin with my finger. "You didn't fail me. He was crazy, Calix. If you'd found him, there's no telling what he would have done to you. Hurt you or worse. I don't know what I would have done if he'd hurt you."

He shakes his head, refusing to look into my eyes. "Emery, do you not see? I healed you, only to strand you here. Without the terrainster, there is no way back to the facility. We are stranded here. Potentially forever."

"I'd rather be stranded with you, than anywhere else without you."

He finally looks up at me. "I promise you I will figure out a way to get us back to safety."

"No," I say firmly. "We'll do it together. I've been a

drain on you long enough. I'm strong now, I can do my part. We're a team. We'll work together or not at all."

Finally, the tension eases from his face. He grins. "I was wrong. You are not a fragile lilapetal, you're a dizmonyx. Rare and strong."

## [ 14 ]
## CALIX

SEVERAL MONTHS LATER

I WATCH my mate as she tears another bright purple leaf from the cabbus ball into a bowl. I am amused because she insists we eat what she calls "cabbage" at least one meal each solar. Even though I am not particularly fond of the flavor, I eat it because she prepares it. I eat it because it is what she craves. Lox had his Haxinth addiction. Breccan had the sun. My mate loves cabbus leaves. I'm grateful that unlike their unhealthy needs, the cabbus ball leaves are packed with nutrients that mimic that of meat, something she does not get much of at all.

As she continues to peel all the good leaves from

the cabbus ball, turning her fingernails the same purple color, I admire her work. She has taken one of the old rooms and converted it into her work space. Many different plants grow in bins lining the walls. I love how she has taken to learn the different plant species of our planet. Plants that grow in the depths of the caves and others that came from seedlings she discovered on one of our many journeys through Sector 1779 searching for useful items.

This is our home.

For now.

And we make the best of it.

Emery keeps us fed while I keep us safe and healthy. While she "gardens" as she calls it, I ensure Sector 1779 is secure. Most recently, upon worries of Lox deciding to show back up, I installed an alarm. We even have a safe space Emery is to hide in if the alarm goes off.

I admire her for a moment longer. She is no longer frail and weak. My mate no longer wears her zuta-metal bracelet that marks her as a sick, weak being. No, since her surgery, she removed the bracelet and has embraced her new, healthy life. Her hips have widened, her thighs have thickened, and her breasts have swelled. My cock jolts at the thought. Slipping from the room, undetected, I head back to my lab. Now is not the time for making love. We both have jobs to do. The mating can wait until tonight when we are too exhausted to do anything aside from losing ourselves in each other.

Back in my lab that has been set up much like my old one at the facility, I head over to my micro-viewer. I have been testing the toxica properties against what I now call the opasites—the gray parasites I removed from Emery's lungs. I have studied the biological code of both, pulling out what makes them different and using the toxica against the opasites. Toxica has a biogene within it that the opasites react negatively to. I've isolated this biogene and strengthened it with newer microbot technology to create a super biogene. This super biogene kills the opasite immediately. Even Emery has been helpful in this effort to protect us from future opasite infections. She explained what she called immunizations from her planet in great detail. The science makes sense and it is my hope to create a lasting agent that can be injected into both morts and our aliens that will protect from future opasite infections.

After a quick check of the time, I head for the comms system. Without fail, I send out a broadcast every solar at the same time in hopes Breccan and the others can hear my messages. I never receive feedback, but I try each solar nonetheless. I have warned them of Lox, told them of the success of Emery's surgery, and that we are safe and healthy. I have told them numerous times that until this massive storm that is looking to last an entire revolution moves on, we will most likely be stuck here. There are solars I long to put my nog together with Avrell or Breccan to discuss important issues, but mostly I am satisfied being here uninterrupted with my mate.

"This is Calix, acting commander of Sector 1779. Do you read me?"

Silence.

"All is well in our Sector. I apologize on our failure to bring back the supplies you had requested. While there is certain technology here that could be useful, there is nothing that you do not already have at the facility. Galen, if you are listening, cabbus ball is a great source of nutrition for the females. It is not something us morts usually choose to eat, but it is incredibly palatable for the females. Have Hadrian search the underground wells." That young mort can barely sit still and since he is Aria's hand, this duty should go to him. The image of him crawling around on the cave floors is amusing to me. "The ground is soft there and cabbus balls could be growing there. If they are, boil them and sprinkle sodiumchloridus crumbs." I chuckle. "Trust me when I say Aria will enjoy this." I let out a sigh and scan my lab. There is always so much to do and work on. "Jareth, if you are listening, I could really use you. Some of the metals around here are old and outdated. I would love to repurpose them but don't have your skillset. Perhaps you can get Ozias to finally fix the comms system so we can speak." I pull off my spectacles and pinch the bridge of my nose. "I miss you morts. All of you. Even Draven's surly self."

It is true. I would give anything to sit around the table with Breccan at the head and Draven standing nearby, leading our charge of morts. To watch Jareth and Sayer doodle notes back and forth to each other. To listen to Avrell excitedly tell us about a new medical breakthrough. To watch Hadrian bounce up and down in his seat like a mortyoung even though he is bigger than most of us old morts. To marvel over Oz and Theron's newest tweak to the *Mayvina*. To sit beside Galen in his always filthy lab coat and discuss plants with him, for once not being put off by the thought of bacteria crawling all over him.

"I must sign off for now. Much work is to be done. I miss you all and hope to see you again one solar soon."

I click off the comms system and let out a heavy sigh. When two small hands grip my shoulders, I do not jolt in surprise but instead lean back. Emery is a miracle worker with her hands. She has a way of kneading my knotted muscles back into a relaxed state.

"You know where those hands always lead us," I say in warning.

She laughs. "Maybe that was the plan all along."

We have been stranded here for many micro-revolutions, or months as Emery calls them, and we have fallen into a bit of a routine. Some solars, though, Emery mixes it up and things get a little filthy.

I do not even shudder anymore.

Once, I took her against the floor in her plant room as her dirty fingernails clawed at me. It was quick and crazed, but I had loved every second of it. Not once did I fret over microorganisms.

She swivels me in my chair until I am facing her. My gaze skims over her beautiful features. Eyes so blue. A pert nose. Always rosy cheeks and the poutiest lips ever. I love how with time, her cheeks are no longer hollow and her skin is never blue.

Tugging her to me, I pull her into my lap so she straddles me. I am always hard and ready to go in her presence. This solar is no different. My cock aches and throbs where she sits on it.

"Any luck on the comms?" she asks, her finger pushing my hair from my eyes. Since we have taken up residence here, I have not cut it. I thought about it, but Emery seems to play with it more the longer it gets. I am quite fond of the relaxing way it feels to have her fingers scratching along my scalp. Pretty soon, I will have hair to my shoulders like Theron.

"No luck," I tell her, my hands finding her fleshy bottom and squeezing. "How are the plants?"

Her blue eyes light up. It is times like these I really do wish we were back at the facility. Galen could teach her so much. Often, she has sat on the comms asking questions to him. No responses ever.

"The cabbage is great. I put some on the stove for supper. And I've been trying a little cross breeding between two of the fruits." She bites on her bottom lip in a shy way. "I don't know if it will work, but it's just a test."

I am proud of how well she has acclimated to this planet, to this Sector, to me. We are home to her. "As long as it does not include any grenus root, I think we are good."

Not long after Lox left, I eradicated the Sector of the root. It is too dangerous. And when hunting within the caves for useful plants and such, I pointed out to Emery the unsafe plants, including the grenus root.

"We have had enough crazy for one lifetime," she says with a smile. "I wouldn't touch that with a ten-foot pole."

I do not know what a ten-foot pole is exactly, but she loves to say those words when referencing things she does not want any part of.

"How long until supper?" I ask as my palms roam to my favorite part of her. Her stomach.

She chuckles. "Soon, for Hope's sake. She's hungry."

We do not have a wegloscan at Sector 1779 to detect pregnancy and the sex, but there is no doubting that Emery is carrying my mortyoung. Not even two micro-revolutions of our being here, she began to present symptoms. Illness in the mornings. Tenderness to her breasts. And she was no longer cycling. She was so sure while I remained hesitant to hope. Then, she started to grow. Lately, I can feel tiny nudges.

Hope.

All we had was hope. All we need is Hope.

"What if it is a boy?" I ask, loving to tease her. She is so certain it is a girl.

Her smile drops a little and tears shine in her eyes. "I thought we could name him Hophalix."

My own heart stutters in my chest. "Hope and Phalix."

She nods. "It was hope that got us here and your father's notes that made Hope possible."

Without his notes, I would've never been able to surgically remove those opasites from her lungs. My mind grows foggy as I think about the early solars here. When I spent countless hours watching the opasites under the micro-viewer. They were living organisms. Parasites of some sort. Their age determined that they were not old. My best guess is she picked them up on the prison ship—most likely inhaled when she took her medicine or possibly ingested them. These notes, too, have been sent through the comms system to the facility.

"Anything new to add to the book?" she asks as she slides out of my lap and walks over to my desk. She thumbs through my notes with interest.

Our book has documented everything we have studied and learned here at Sector 1779. All information we have relayed back to the facility. I am not sure they have heard a word of it, but if they have not, these notes will be here for the next mort who comes along long after we are gone.

Her scent—a scent I have come to learn becomes headier when her body requires mine to mate with—permeates the air. Once we make love, the scent dissipates considerably. She says going too long without having me makes me smell good, too. Of course, I had to understand why this is. After running some tests, her enzymes seem to weaken when we haven't made love. The moment my toxica hits her system, it repairs the weakening enzymes and gives her a boost of good health. She calls it sexual prenatal vitamins. I know it is more than a silly name she calls it. The toxica is good for the womb is my best guess, although I would love to run the idea by Avrell.

"Do you think Aria has had the baby yet?" Emery asks, dragging me from my thoughts.

I calculate the time of gestation and our time here. It is getting close. "Perhaps. Or soon."

She turns to face me. "And you are sure you will be able to deliver ours?"

Flashing her a smug grin, I nod. "I taught Avrell just about everything he knows. We studied the same manuals. I know we can do this."

"Me too—"

Her words are cut off by the blaring of an alarm. It sends a chill or terror running down my spine. Emery's eyes are wide with fright.

"To the safe place," I bark as I jump from my seat and take off in a sprint.

I hear a door slam shut behind me as she seeks her hiding spot. I run toward the weapons wall and snag one of the sharpest spears. One of Emery's other favorite things to do is whittle dizmonyx gems from the cavern walls. Then, after dinner some evenings, we fashion them into weapons. With Lox on the loose, you can never be too sure.

Because there is so much to do here, and I do not spend as much time as I used to locked in a lab like back at the facility, I have grown stronger. Emery is carrying my mortyoung and I have insisted she grow stronger too. Together, we build our strength and have been working on endurance. One solar, when the storm has cleared, we will make that trek back to the facility. And when we do, we will need to be at optimal physical health.

I can hear a banging sound as though someone is trying to break through the door. It is not accompanied with scratches or growls, indicating a sabrevipe. My sub-bones pop and crack as I ready myself for what's behind the door.

Many solars, I have lain in our bed in the dark and thought of how I will end Lox. I want vengeance for what he did to my father. When the time arrives, I will not hesitate. There will be no reform cell with his name on it. Only The Eternals—the place where all morts go once they leave this life. His life here is over.

I take a moment to throw on some zu-gear over my

minnasuit. I may be eager to get my hands on the mad rekking mort, but I will not expose myself in the process. Once I'm suited up, I unlock the chamber door and yank my arm back, ready to fire my spear at him.

The door is shoved open and I am attacked right away. The wild mort charges at me, my spear whizzing past him. It snaps in half as the chamber door closes back on its own with a clang, making him flinch at the sound.

Rekk!

We scuffle and roll. Each throwing punches. When did Lox get so strong? He is an old mort and I should be able to take him. Yet here he is—heavy and powerful.

"Stop!" the voice barks from behind the mask.

But I don't stop. I pummel him with my fists until he has them pushed down to the floor. Rage consumes me. I'm able to roll him over and pin him. My eyes frantically search the space for a weapon. I notice a magknife strapped to his side and fumble for it.

"Would you rekking stop?" he snarls from behind his mask.

His voice is familiar and it has me faltering. Enough so that he rolls us again. I'm pinned once more. He yanks off his mask and my eyes lock with a pair of wild eyes all right. Wild eyes I have watched for many, many revolutions. Wild eyes I have studied. Wild eyes I have wanted to help.

The alarm that has been blaring in the background goes silent, echoing still in my head.

And then I see even wilder eyes behind him. Blue ones. Protective and fierce. My mate grabs a handful of this mort's patchy hair and yanks his nog back, a carpal knife at his throat. He gapes at me in surprise.

"Emery," I say slowly. "Let him go. It is okay, lilapetal."

She blinks several times. "L-Lox will k-kill you if I d-do."

"It is a good thing this is not Lox," I say, grinning at her. "This is our friend, Draven."

My expression must put her at ease because she steps back, the carpal knife still gripped tight in her tiny fist as she cradles her swollen stomach. Draven rolls away from me and is on his feet in the next moment. His eyes dart to the door and he backs his body that way, keeping us at his front.

"Is that how you greet all your guests, mortarekker?" he grumbles.

I rise to my feet and pull Emery close to me. "You are our first one, so I suppose the answer is yes." A grin stretches across my face. "How the rekk are you? Why are you here?"

His tense shoulders relax and he unzips out of his zu-gear. He has a satchel strapped to him against his minnasuit. From inside the satchel he pulls out a book. It looks familiar. Like those Sayer is always scribbling away in.

"The comms system works," Draven grunts. "Well, apparently only one way." He scrubs at his scarred face and gives me a withering look. "You really should turn it off when you mate your female."

Emery lets out a surprised squeak. "You heard us have sex?"

I let out a rumble of laughter. "We shall be more careful next time."

Draven's brows furrow. "Next time? There won't be a next time. You're coming back with me. This is a rescue mission."

I shake my head. "We are not going."

Draven frowns. "Breccan was afraid you were going to say that."

"She is carrying my mortyoung, Draven. Too fragile to risk a long journey, even via a terrainster." I kiss the top of my mate's nog. "I won't leave her. One solar, we will return."

"Very well," Draven says, holding out the book he has brought.

I take it from his grip. Flipping through it, I am amazed at all the notes. From everyone. Detailed notes from Galen about plants. A whole section from Ozias on how to repair the comms system. I am pleased to find some useful information from Avrell about birthing a mortyoung. There is plenty to read, so I simply skim through it before closing it. "What is all this?"

"All your questions answered. Sayer stays on the comms. Since you make communication at the same time each solar, we don't miss your broadcasts. He's been gathering all the information you needed. Breccan wanted me to bring you two back, but Avrell worried your mate might be pregnant by now. That book is what Aria calls 'the insurance policy.' Whatever the rekk that means."

"It means," Emery says as she takes the book from me. "They wanted us to come back, but in case we couldn't, there was a backup plan to keep us safe and informed." She giggles. "This is amazing."

"Did Lox ever show?" I ask, my blood once again turning to ice.

Draven scowls. "He attempted to steal the *Mayvina*. He did not succeed."

"Is he dead?"

"I rekking wish," he growls. "But, no. He's out there somewhere. It's wise you keep greeting all your guests the way you greeted me." He looks back at the chamber door. "But I'm going to leave you with some better weapons. That rekker isn't suited up like us. He's traipsing around out in the biggest geostorm we've seen in nothing but scraps of a minnasuit. You see him, you shoot him with a zonnoblaster."

"Thank you, Draven," I say. "Will you be staying for some delightful 'cabbage'?"

Emery playfully elbows me, sensing my teasing her.

His lip curls up. "I brought my own rations. I will be staying long enough to help you fix the comms and then I must go. Galen has been watching the geostorm's pattern and we're in for an influx of magnastrikes in the next few solars. I need to be headed back long before then." He snags his helmet up and heads for the chamber door. "Let me unload this gear and we'll get to work."

As soon as he's gone, I take Emery's face in my hands. "All we had to do was hope."

She stands on her toes, her swollen stomach pressing against my firmer one. "Hope hasn't let us down yet."

My lips press to hers and we kiss like there is no tomorrow.

Passionately. Frantically. Endlessly.

But fortunately, for us, we have many more wonderful solars ahead of us. And each morning, I will wake and hope for more.

Hope hasn't let us down yet.

# EPILOGUE
## DRAVEN

THREE SOLARS LATER

I STEP through the decontamination bay still sizzling from a near miss of a magnastrike. My sub-bones feel as though they're alive and crawling with energy from the blinding white of the magnastrike that melted the back of my suit.

I was nearly rekking killed by the elements, and yet it didn't threaten to consume my mind like this facility does. The familiar roaring inside my nog comes raging to the forefront like a pack of hungry sabrevipes eager to feast on my sanity.

*Stop thinking about it.*

My skin crawls as I quickly dart my gaze back at the exit. I can escape if I need to. I'm not trapped here.

I'm not trapped.

I'm not trapped.

I can escape if I want.

Heat, nothing to do with my near miss with the magnastrike, burns through me. This heat was something that caught fire within me when I'd contracted The Rades. With the fire came the maddening thoughts. The voices. The terror. The darkness. The pain.

Inside my chest, my heart is pounding to the point I feel dizzy. The past three solars, aside from the horrible geostorm, were freeing. When Breccan asked for a volunteer to take Calix and his mate the necessary supplies they needed at Sector 1779, I'd jumped so fast at the chance, I made all the morts around me startle.

This place is a prison.

My mind is a prison.

This rekking planet is a prison.

And despite it all, everyone around me seems happy. Hopeful even. When Theron and Sayer brought back the aliens, it was as though all the morts were brought back to life. As though they had purpose again.

Everyone but me.

The arrival of the females only further aggravated

my mind. Their soft, sweet voices remind me of my mother and sister. Of a past where I once laughed and had purpose. I don't laugh anymore. I don't do anything aside from try to live solar by solar. The only time I feel some semblance of peace is when I'm in The Tower. And since this geostorm has been ravaging us for nearly a revolution, I haven't spent any time hardly at all up there. This trapped feeling only intensifies each solar.

At one point, I'd looked at the stars beyond and wondered if I could ride with Theron in the *Mayvina*. Maybe the trapped feeling would lessen if I was off this rekking planet. But all that died when the females arrived. They rooted us here. I can see it in Breccan's eyes. He wants to make Mortuus a real home again. Everyone spends countless hours making new plans on how to make our lives better. They look at the future.

I'm stuck in the past.

So often my mind drifts to those dark times where I was captive to that disease. And despite healing from it physically, it has left its wicked mark on my brain. I'll never be free of The Rades. Rekking never.

I'm tearing off my zu-gear as I leave the rigorous cleansing in the small decontamination bay when Hadrian rounds the corner, eyes wide and excited.

"The mortyoung is coming! You're just in time!" he bellows. "What did you get?"

His fast talking and energetic movements make me tense. I eye the door behind me. So close. Ignoring my urge to flee, I reach into my satchel and bring out Calix's notes.

"The supplies Breccan was hopeful for do not exist. I searched Sector 1779 myself. However, there are important notes that will be helpful. Plus—"

"We can rekking communicate now thanks to you," he says with a crooked grin. "Females talk a lot. Like a lot. I am thankful Aria has another female to yammer to. Usually Breccan feigns 'work' and leaves me to listen to Aria's never ending tales. She and Emery spoke for nearly half a solar over the smell of a mortyoung's hair." He groans. "Hours and hours, Draven."

Hadrian talks more than either female, so I'm not sure what he's complaining about.

I eye the west entrance door again. It's not too late. I could go back to Sector 1779. It was a little quieter there. The trapped feeling wasn't so bad there.

*Boom!*

A loud magnastrike makes the entire facility shake and then we're plunged into total darkness.

I freeze as my heart rate spikes.

I am not trapped. I can escape. Even in the dark. I can get away.

Within seconds, though, everything comes back to life and we're bathed in light once more. I let out a ragged breath of relief.

Aria's pained scream echoes from what must be Avrell's lab. It reminds me too much of my past—when The Rades consumed my rekking everything.

"Go assist," I bark out. "I'll check to make sure everything stays up and running."

He runs off without another word and disappears into Avrell's lab. Usually Oz or Jareth would handle this sort of thing, but I don't want to be anywhere near a screaming female as she delivers her mortyoung. Rekk no.

Instead, I head in the opposite direction, checking rooms as I go. Everything on the south side of the facility is in working order. I pass Avrell's lab and block out the screaming as I head for the north area of the facility where the females' sub-faction exists. When I get a whiff of an electrical burning, I take off running. Even focused on my task ahead of me, I count doors, exits, windows. I've memorized them all in this facility, yet I can't help but check and double-check. When I reach the source of the smell, I let out a hiss of frustration. The cryochamber room. Three cryotube pods remain. I hate going in this room. Seeing them trapped inside makes me panic. The urge to free them is nearly overwhelming. I don't even like them, but I don't want them trapped. If anyone knows how horrible it feels to be trapped, it's me.

But the last time one was hastily freed, she nearly died. Aria yanked Emery out and it caused an uproar within our ranks. It was voted that they will remain there, sleeping, until it can be decided on when and how to safely wake them.

Slowly, I walk into the room. Smoke comes from one of the cryotubes. I detach the wires from the standing pod, grab one of the misters, and douse the flames before they can spread.

*Pop.*

*Hiss.*

Those two sounds send alarm racing through me. Without thinking, I did exactly what I've been told not to do.

Don't wake them.

I scramble away from the cryotube now that the fire is safely put out and rush to the east door of the cryochamber room. The cool air on the back of my neck—the feel of freedom just behind me—calms me considerably.

I will tell Breccan the geostorm electrical surge caused it.

I will lie.

His warnings to put anyone who messes with the cryotubes into a reform cell has my entire body trembling. When I was eaten up with The Rades, I was forced into one. To protect me from myself. To protect others from me.

I can't go back there.

Not now. Not ever.

Turning, I decide to bolt. But a sound stops me.

Whimpering at first.

Then crying.

Sad, fearful crying.

RUN!

RUNRUNRUNRUN!

And yet my useless boots stay planted to the ground. The lid of the cryotube creaks open. I'm frozen in horror as the alien climbs out of the pod trembling badly. Her hair is like the other two aliens if you were to mix them together. Light, the color of the sun, on top, and dark underneath. It hangs in long, messy waves, covering her breasts. She's not as small as the other two aliens. Her bones are larger. She carries more meat. Maybe this one is stronger. Maybe I won't have hurt her.

Her nog darts all around as she takes in the space, her gaze falling first on the door behind me and then a quick look at the west door behind her. Then, her eyes meet mine. Brown eyes. Wide. Terrified. Spilling liquid. She takes a step toward me, her bottom lip trembling. I take a step back. When she reaches her hand forward, I take another step back.

"H-Help me," she croaks.

She steps forward again and again and again. I stumble back until I crash against the wall beside the door.

Trapped.

My head darts left and then to just behind her. Exits on two sides of this room.

RUN!

And then her declawed fingers clutch onto my bare arms. All of my minnasuits have been modified to keep my arms free of anything that will touch and chafe my scars. She clings to me, her naked front pressing against me, and I choke on my terror.

I'm trapped.

I'm rekking trapped.

Everything turns black.

I go down and take the alien with me.

Helpmehelpmehelpme.

Those words are hers or mine or both.

I don't know.

I don't know.

I don't rekking know.

I'm trapped.

"Help me."

This time, I know it's me.

I'm pleading for anyone who will listen.

The black is swirling around me as my world spins. Her breath is hot near my neck, scalding me. Her words mirror mine. The darkness steals me this time, our words echoing back and forth into nothingness.

"Help me."

I'm trapped.

There is no getting away.

This alien will be the death of me.

*Keep reading with the next installment...*
*THE MAD LIEUTENANT!*

## ACKNOWLEDGMENTS

K WEBSTER

Thank you to my husband. You're my favorite weirdo! I love you bunches!

I want to give a huge thanks to Nicole Blanchard for being so mortarekking awesome! Your love for aliens matches only that of my own! So proud to have created this world with you and can't wait to write many more stories!

A huge thank you to my Krazy for K Webster's Books reader group. You all are insanely supportive and I can't thank you enough.

A gigantic thank you to those who always help me out. Elizabeth Clinton, Ella Stewart, Misty Walker, Holly Sparks, Jillian Ruize, Gina Behrends, Rosa

Saucedo, Jessica Hollyfield, Ker Dukey, and Nikki Ash —you ladies are my rock!

Thank you so much to Misty for helping me with EVERYTHING and ALL the time!  You're the best sister from another mister!

A big thank you to my author friends who have given me your friendship and your support. You have no idea how much that means to me.

Thank you to all of my blogger friends both big and small that go above and beyond to always share my stuff. You all rock! #AllBlogsMatter

Emily A. Lawrence, thank you SO much for editing these aliens. You're amazing and I can't thank you enough! Love you!

Lastly but certainly not least of all, thank you to all of the wonderful readers out there who are willing to hear my story and enjoy my characters like I do. It means the world to me!

NICOLE BLANCHARD

If I were stranded on a lost planet I'd want to drag the following people along with me:

My kiddo, the pain in my neck. The sunshine in my life. You make everything worth it.

My boyfriend Charlie, who always makes life a little sweeter.

K Webster, of course, because who else shares my love of aliens? Honestly, let's just run off to Mortuus right now! I look forward to many, many more stories together.

The entire Nicole's Knockouts group. I am always humbled by your support and encouragement. Thank you for being by my side all these years.

Melissa Fisher and Alana Albertson—I couldn't finish a book without you so clearly I'd have to drag you along.

Emily A. Lawrence—thank you for making our aliens shine!

Last, but certainly not least, all of my wonderful readers. You ROCK!

 **K Webster** is the author of dozens of romance books in many different genres including contemporary romance, historical romance, paranormal romance, and erotic romance. When not spending time with her husband of twelve years and two adorable children, she's active on social media connecting with her readers. Her other passions besides writing include reading and graphic design. K can always be found in front of her computer chasing her next idea and taking action. She looks forward to the day when she will see one of her titles on the big screen.

facebook.com/authorkwebster

twitter.com/KristiWebster

instagram.com/authorkwebster

amazon.com/K-Webster

bookbub.com/authors/k-webster

goodreads.com/K_Webster

**War & Peace Series**

Box Set

This is War, Baby

This is Love, Baby

This Isn't Over, Baby

This Isn't You, Baby

This is Me, Baby

This Isn't Fair, Baby

This is the End, Baby

**Taboo Treats**

Bad Bad Bad

Easton

Lawn Boys

Malfeasance

Mr. Blakely

Renner's Rules

Ex-Rated Attraction

Coach Long

The Glue

Dane

Enzo

Red Hot Winter

## Pretty Dolls Series

Pretty Stolen Dolls

Pretty Lost Dolls

Pretty New Doll

Pretty Broken Doll

## The V Games

Vlad

Ven

Vas

## 2 Lovers Series

Text 2 Lovers

Hate 2 Lovers

Thieves 2 Lovers

## The Lost Planet Series

The Forgotten Commander

The Vanished Specialist

The Mad Lieutenant

**Breaking the Rules Series**

Box Set

Blue Christmas

Broken

Wrong

Scarred

Mistake

Crushed

**The Vegas Aces**

Box Set

Rock Country

Rock Heart

Rock Bottom

**Alpha & Omega**

Alpha & Omega

Omega & Love

## Becoming Her

Box Set

Becoming Mrs. Benedict

Becoming Lady Thomas

Becoming Countess Dumont

## Four Fathers

Pearson

## Four Sons

Camden

## Woodland Creek

Running Free

## Standalones

Apartment 2B

Love and Law

Moth to a Flame

Erased

The Road Back to Us

B-Sides and Rarities

Sweet Jayne

Untimely You

Notice

The Day She Cried

My Torin

Surviving Harley

Schooled by a Senior

Whispers and the Roars

Dirty Ugly Toy

Give Me Yesterday

Sundays are for Hangovers

El Malo

Mad Sea

Blue Hill Blood

Sunshine and the Stalker

The Wild

Hale

Cold Cole Heart

Heath

Like Dragonflies

**Nicole Blanchard** is the *New York Times* and *USA Today* best-selling author of gritty romantic suspense and heartwarming new adult romance. She and her family reside in the south along with their two spunky Boston Terriers and one chatty cat. Visit her website www.authornicoleblanchard.com for more information or to subscribe to her newsletter for updates on sales and new releases.

facebook.com/authornicoleblanchard

twitter.com/blanchardbooks

instagram.com/authornicoleblanchard

amazon.com/Nicole-Blanchard

bookbub.com/authors/nicole-blanchard

goodreads.com/nicole_blanchard

## The Lost Planet Series

The Forgotten Commander

The Vanished Specialist

The Mad Lieutenant

## Immortals Ever After Series

Deal with a Dragon

Vow to a Vampire

Fated to a Fae King

## Dark Romance

Toxic

Fatal

## Standalone Novellas

Bear with Me

Darkest Desires

Mechanical Hearts

55405351R00124

Made in the USA
Columbia, SC
13 April 2019